The Bite
and other Apocryphal Tales

FRANCIS GREIG

The Bite
and other
Apocryphal Tales

JONATHAN CAPE
THIRTY BEDFORD SQUARE LONDON

First published 1981
Copyright © 1981 by Francis Greig
Jonathan Cape Ltd, 30 Bedford Square, London WC1

British Library Cataloguing in Publication Data

Greig, Francis
  The bite and other apocryphal tales
  1. Tales, English
  I. Title
  398.2'1'0942   GR141
  ISBN 0-224-01904-X

Typeset by Inforum Ltd, Portsmouth
Printed in Great Britain by St Edmundsbury Press
Bury St Edmunds, Suffolk

This book is dedicated to the people in whose houses much of it was written:

Michael and Sybil Brown
Colonel and Madame LeGuennec
Clarence Paget
John and Beryl Tough
George and Joan Turnbull

and to Paul Morris, who was kind enough to read the tales piecemeal and tactful enough to like them

Contents

Introduction

' There are a terrible lot of lies going about the world,' an anonymous Irishman once said, 'and half of them are true.' Apocryphal tales are an indelible part of modern folklore: as much a factor in everyday life as jokes or gossip. Their familiarity lies in the likelihood that most of us will, at some time or another, have been told such a story, recognizing in it events we have heard of before − slightly altered in detail, perhaps, but unchanged in essence. Their peculiarity has to do with the fact that they are invariably presented as true: whoever is telling the story will have heard it from a friend who knows the person it happened to, or will have read a newspaper report of it, or have learned of it in some other way. There is never any suggestion that the tale is other than completely factual.

I'm not suggesting for a moment that people who repeat these stories are liars; far from it. On a number of occasions when I've been told about a frightening or bizarre event that happened to 'a friend's friend', and have been unable to keep myself from identifying the story as apocryphal, the person telling the tale has insisted that it is true and can be verified. There is something in the nature of an apocryphal story that makes it believable − or that makes us want to believe it. And why shouldn't we? The fact that we recognize events that are supposed to have happened only a few days ago as being identical to those in a story told years before doesn't mean that those events *never* occurred; it does mean, though, that they remain relevant to us: have about them something of a basic fear, or a fundamental attraction, that finds a universal response. Viewed in that light, the apocryphal story becomes even more intriguing. It is not surprising, perhaps, that most of them tend to be wry, or sinister, or macabre.

This collection gathers together a number of stories that I have heard many times: and each time offered as the truth by someone who quite clearly believed . . . was prepared to believe . . . every word. My purpose has been to assume the truth for each tale: to re-create it, building on the factors common to each telling, providing character and motive and incident, in order to give a notion of what might have happened that *first* time, before the people and events were absorbed by our unconscious minds and made anonymous by repetition. And, of course, many people reading the stories will say, 'That one's definitely not invented − I know someone who knows the person it happened to.' Because it's very possible that *all* of them are true.

London, 1981   F.G.

The Hitch-hiker

It had been touch and go whether Carole Phillips would reach the London main-line station in time to catch the last train. She had worked very late that night, preparing a report on the small department she managed in the London office of a textile manufacturer; and, since she would be too late and too tired to cook when she arrived home, had gone to a small restaurant for a salad before looking for a taxi to take her to the station.

The service at the restaurant had been slow and when she left the place a slight drizzle had begun to fall: enough to make taxis irritatingly scarce. Finally, though, she flagged one down and sat on the edge of her seat as it dragged through traffic towards the station. She made the train with seconds to spare and fell against the buttoned upholstery, recovering slowly from her sprint through the station concourse.

During the seventy-minute trip to the Home Counties town where she lived, she looked up from her book now and then to peer out of the window into the darkness. The rain had quickened. Heavy drops, blown into a spread of wet lace, hung on the glass. Beyond, she could see the black shadows of trees alongside the line stirring in the wind; and

1

behind the trees the indistinct, sodden fields lit along their edges by the lights from the carriages. She reflected that even the tamest countryside can seem intimidating at night: and especially in bad weather. Out there in the blackness, predators were closing in on their prey — ruthlessly, silently. In those apparently empty fields, sudden attacks were taking place; there were tiny, unheard screams of pain; there was blood and violent death, the killer standing above its victim as the little corpse still quivered in its grip. This late at night, the normally tolerable commuting trip could seem endless.

By the time she reached her destination, the weather had become wild. The rain had thinned, but was carried almost horizontally by a harsh, cold wind that buffeted her as she struggled along the platform. She was the only passenger to alight. Her heeltaps rang on the flagstones, seeming to sing, like asdic, as if they were finding a resonance below the surface. She always felt slightly at risk when coming home on the last train — silly, of course; a hangover from childhood fears of the dark, of the bogeyman, of the imagined figure at the top of the stairs. Even so, she never felt quite safe until she had crossed the car-park and (feeling a bit foolish) locked herself into the car before starting off.

As usual, this late at night, there was no one on duty to take her ticket. A light burned dimly in one of the station rooms, but whoever was in there either hadn't noticed that a passenger had got off the train, or didn't care. She pushed her season-ticket back into her pocket and took out her car keys.

She had arrived at the station that morning with only a few minutes to spare: cutting things fine is a characteristic of the practised commuter. So her car had been parked among the furthest from the entrance, although now it was the only vehicle left there beneath the row of tossing yew trees that bordered the fence.

The car-park was no more than a large, cordoned-off area

2

of bare earth, rutted and strewn with cinders for drainage — unlit and far from the sparse street-lamps lining the country road by the station approach. She crossed the sixty yards or so of rough ground at a fast pace, her coat flapping in the wind. Once she stumbled in a deep rut and almost loosed her hold on the car keys — that would have been a disaster, she thought, since it was too dark to see more than a few feet ahead. She knew exactly where the car was, though, and walked unfalteringly to it. As she put the key in the lock, she heard a quiet voice from out of the blackness, directly behind her.

For a second her heart seemed to stop entirely. Then her brain began to function, offering reassurance: it had been a woman's voice. Even so, she turned to face the voice's owner with fear curdling in her stomach; but as the person came a little closer, she relaxed. A woman stood there, dressed rather shabbily in a worn top-coat and a felt hat. Her hair was grey, she was clearly in late-middle age, and she seemed to be upset.

'Excuse me, Miss,' she repeated the words that the girl had first heard.

'What's wrong?' Clearly something must be wrong. Why else would this old dear be standing in a station car-park at midnight enduring a half-gale?

'Can you help me? It's so silly. I arranged for a taxi to meet me from my train and it's not here. I thought your car might be it and that the driver would come back, but I've been waiting for ages. Are you going towards town?'

'Yes. I'm going into the town.' The girl began to feel distinctly sorry for the old lady. To be stuck out at the station — a four-mile bus or cab ride from the town — waiting for transport that obviously wasn't going to come almost put her in the category of distressed gentleperson. 'Where do you live?'

'Well, it's on that road — almost in the town itself. You could very nearly drop me at my door without going out of

3

your way. Would you mind?'

The girl unlocked the car and got in, then lifted the catch on the passenger-door to admit the old lady. When they were both settled, the girl leaned over and opened the glove-compartment on the passenger's side. She kept a wooden clothes-peg in there: her unscientific but effective method for keeping the erratic choke out long enough to get the car going. She had just retrieved the peg, when she happened to glance down. She froze. The illumination from the glove-compartment revealed that the backs of her passenger's hands — which were neatly folded in her lap — were covered in a thick growth of dark hairs!

The girl's mind screamed at her: *It's a man! Oh, my God, it's a man!* Somehow, she managed to remain outwardly calm, fiddling with this or that control while her brain raced, desperately trying to improvise an escape. By some means, she had to get the person out of the car.

Without pegging the choke back, she turned the ignition key, knowing that the car wouldn't start. Three or four times she made a show of doing this, pretending to get more annoyed. Hoping that her voice wouldn't quaver, she said, 'Oh dear! It does this sometimes. Usually, I have to get a push.' Then she turned the key twice more, to no effect.

'Damn!' She chewed her lip as if searching for a solution. 'Look, it's an awful thing to ask, but I don't see how else we're going to get the wretched car started. We're on a bit of a hill here. If you could just give it a tiny push to start it off, it'll roll down the slope and I can get the engine going. Would you?'

Somewhat to her surprise, her passenger agreed. Maybe the light in the station — impossibly far as a refuge, but close enough to make a potential attacker feel uneasy. — had influenced the matter. Anyway, the girl waited, breathlessly, as the passenger-door closed and the figure went around to the back of the car. Instantly, she snapped down the inside locks, jammed the peg behind the choke-rod,

4

started the car, roared across the car-park, along the station approach and on to the road.

After a mile or so, the mad fluttering of the girl's heart slowed. The whole incident seemed dream-like. She could hardly believed it had really happened — though if she needed to assure herself that it had, she had the evidence of the handbag that the old lady had left on the floor of the car when she got out. In fact, it may have been the handbag that first caused the girl to wonder whether she mightn't have acted rather hastily. Had she perhaps just swept out of the car-park leaving behind a thoroughly confused old lady who simply happened to have rather hairy hands? After all, some women were unlucky that way and only the young would bother to do something about the condition. More than that, the light from the glove-compartment might have made the hairiness look worse than it was. What evidence did she have? Almost none. She was aware, though, that her natural nervousness, her slight fear of the dark and the wild weather might have prompted her to act stupidly. If she *had* made a mistake, then she had driven off with the poor woman's handbag. But still she remembered those *very* hairy hands!

By the time she reached town, she was in a terrible quandary about the whole incident. Had she just survived an encounter with a homicidal maniac or had her irrational fear led her to act in a terribly unkind manner? Either way, she decided, her best course of action was to go to the local police station. The person she had just abandoned would need to be either rescued or investigated.

As she told her story to the sergeant on duty, she became increasingly sure in her own mind that she had acted cruelly and stupidly. It *had* been an old lady; hairy hands were no sign of malice; and she had left her out there at the station with no means of getting home.

She said as much to the sergeant, who agreed that it was probably the case. 'I'll send someone out there,' he told the

5

girl. 'In the meantime, we'd better have a look in her hand-bag to find out who she is in case she's left the station.'

Together, they went out to the car. The girl produced the bag – a large soft-leather affair with a swivel clasp – and handed it to the sergeant, who snapped open the clasp and held the bag open so that they could both see what it held.

The sergeant's exclamation was followed by a small shriek from the girl; she staggered slightly and seemed about to faint, so that the policeman had to support her by an arm. The shaft of the axe had been sawn short so that it would fit into the bag. It was the only thing in there, and the honed cutting edge shone along its bevelled length in the white lamp-light.

The Street Cries
of Old London

It was Monday and so, in accordance with Martin's rota system, Paul would sit in the hand-cart, Julian and Tricia would pull it, Ben would tag along behind and Martin himself would hold the woollen ski-hat and collect the money. Martin's father had supplied the hat and started them off with a fistful of small change so that there would be something to jingle.

The whole scheme had been Martin's idea. To begin with, his father had been opposed to it, but the children, together with Martin's mother, had managed to talk him round.

'I'm not at all sure I approve,' he had said at first. 'It's always seemed like begging to me.' Martin's mother was lifting the Sunday roast out of the oven and transferring it to a carving dish; she took a quick swig of wine. 'Nonsense, darling,' she chided. 'Do the gravy will you?' Martin sat quietly on the sofa, leafing through the colour supplements. He knew that, with his mother on his side, the battle was as good as won.

'Well, what about his homework? And have the other parents given their permission?'

'Yes, so I gather.' She half-carved a slice of the lamb to make sure it wasn't bloody. 'Don't worry. Homework won't be skimped. It's not as if they were collecting for themselves. I'd tend to agree with you if they were collecting for themselves. I think it's a tremendously good idea — shows thoughtfulness and initiative.'

After lunch, Martin asked if he might be allowed to go round to Julian's house: to finalize their plans, he said. He put on his mac because it was drizzling slightly, then hung around by the kitchen door while his parents stacked the dishes and began the washing-up.

'O.K.' His father turned on the kitchen taps and squeezed some washing-up liquid into the bowl. 'I suppose it's all right. One proviso: I want you to be back, each evening, no later than half-past five and you're to finish your homework before dinner.' He lowered the first batch of plates into the soapy water. 'Now, have you got the whole thing organized properly?'

On his way to Julian's house, Martin smiled as he reflected on his father's final question. It was just like him to want to organize things once he had given his permission. There was no need, though. Tricia had supplied the little hand-cart for the guy to sit in, Ben's mother had adapted an old suit so that it would fit the children and help them to look the part; she, too, had fixed ragged straw hair round the inside of an ancient trilby and glued more clumps of straw to the sleeves and turn-ups of the suit, using what was left to decorate the jumble-sale waistcoat that completed the outfit. When Ben tried it all on — allowed to have first go, since his mother had created it — the other children agreed that it was Worzel Gummidge to the life. They were sufficiently sophisticated to know that a TV character would be better for their cause than just any old guy. The only unauthentic touch, perhaps, was the plastic mask they had purchased from a local toy-shop. It was a grinning, snub-nosed, rosy-cheeked face and didn't fit the role that well: but it was the best they could find.

The idea had occurred to Martin during a morning assembly the week before. The children had been asked to bring to school any toys or books that they had finished with, so that these could be passed on to the local orphanage. Martin's school had a special connection with the orphanage. The large, gabled, red-brick building was no more than two streets away from Hillview Middle School and every weekday at twelve-thirty the orphanage children would line up in a crocodile and walk to Hillview for lunch — a local councillor had devised the notion as a means of cutting the orphanage's overheads. Four tables in the Hillview canteen were set aside for the orphans and there, each schoolday, they sat, looking a little embarrassed and sullen (or so it seemed to Martin), ordered to be on their best behaviour until the time came to form up again and march through the playground. The Hillview children would line up themselves to watch them depart, trying to imagine what it would be like to have no mother and no father but only — and endlessly — teachers.

Martin had decided that he and his friend should collect 'pennies for the guy' — the proceeds to go to the orphans as a contribution towards fireworks for Guy Fawkes Night. In truth, there wasn't a deeply philanthropic feeling behind the plan; more an excitement at the notion of taking turns to dress up and sit in the hand-cart, or of vying with each other to see who could collect the most money. That they were collecting for 'a good cause' was altogether secondary, though it allowed them to feel a little self-righteous.

Martin had decided, too, that they would have a human guy, rather than the misshapen bundle of rag-stuffed sacking that usually served. It would give them the edge over any other collectors as well as being something of a novelty. They made great efforts — or, rather, Ben's mother made great efforts under the children's instruction — to disguise the fact that the figure in the hand-cart was anything but a very superior model of a guy. Each took turns rehearsing the role — slumping crookedly in the cart, one arm dang-

9

ling, head thrown back or tilted to one side, legs trailing over the front edge. Tricia came up with the idea of shallow breathing, to reduce the rise and fall of the guy's chest. After several 'goes' apiece, they agreed that each made a pretty good job of being a dummy.

There had been a slight squabble about who should have first turn; that was when Martin had made them draw straws and then written up a rota based on the results. No one, however, had argued about the collecting site. They would stand outside Thompson's the Butcher's. Anyone who was collecting for anything stood there: it was the obvious place, in the middle of the High Street and right on the crossroads with George Street. People passed to and fro constantly, going from one shop to another, using the zebra crossing, making for the department store at the lower end of George Street or the baker's at the upper end, or walked along the High Street on their way to Woolworth's or the supermarket. The RSPCA lady collected there, the poppy people, the cancer research and lifeboat volunteers. It was the traditional flag-day pitch. The children determined to get there as early as possible after school to stake their claim. It was Monday: Paul's turn to be in the cart.

Distressed spaniels and ill-treated donkeys, the wives of dead heroes, the terminally ill, men who put to sea in a black gale – they were all a source of monumental irritation to Jack Thompson, as were buskers, the distributors of leaflets, and street vendors. Before the town was redeveloped ('ruined' would be the term used by most of the locals), before the advent of 'London overspill', before the High Street had been crammed with jazzy shop-fronts, before the big estates had been thrown up on all sides of the town and a light-engineering industry had taken over from farming as the town's principal employer and the area's ripe vowels had given way to a sort of bastard Cockney – before the existence of the ugly concrete wilderness that the developers referred to as the New Town Centre – flagday operations had always taken place in the old Market Square. Nowadays, the Square was unused: *en route* to nowhere. The cobbles grew little archipelagoes of moss, the wooden Town Hall where the library used to be was abandoned to graffiti, the statue of a Roundhead VIP, dappled with verdigris, looked oddly isolate, as if his troop had deserted.

The collectors' new pitch had become a source of obsession with Jack. He was a conservative man, like his father had been, and ran his shop along conservative lines. There was competition, now, of course; not like the old days. Competition from two other butchers who had bought shops closer to the new estates, competition from the supermarket and its meat-counter, competition from the grocers' and general stores which sold pre-packed ham and bacon from enormous cabinets. Jack sneered at them all. He was a traditional butcher; he cared about his craft and that was why he was so proud of the window: the trays of meat containing prime cuts in their thin swill of blood; the rabbits hanging in neat squads and flanked by pheasants with swooping tail feathers, their eyes filmed-over in death; the dark, dense slabs of liver; the tangle of tripes and seething worms of mince: all were arranged with care and for the best effect. Nearest the window would be earthenware dishes of home-made pâté topped with a crust of butter or glistening under rich jelly; at the back, rammed on to thick steel hooks, the stripped and cloven carcasses of pigs. Each Saturday, without fail, it seemed, someone with a tray and a slotted tin would stand four-square in front of Jack's display. People peered round the intruder to get a look in the window. At any given time, Jack could expect to look up from where he was jointing a rabbit or carving a steak and see, amid the faces looking in, a back resolutely turned towards him and a hand rattling a tin on a cord.

It wasn't just that his window display was partly obscured − though that was infuriating; and not just that

11

people were likely to avoid his shop as they avoided the flag-seller — though Jack was quite sure that he lost a deal of trade that way, arguing that potential customers, whether they were likely to be embarrassed by a lack of small change or not, would probably experience a kind of psychological check when confronted by someone making a demand on them, or pestering them as they approached. No — more than either of these annoyances, Jack was incensed by the sight of that turned back. It seemed a rejection; it seemed arrogant and insulting; it seemed offensively *vegetarian*.

The children arrived at four o'clock. Jack heard a slight scrape and then a knock on the plate-glass as they set the hand-cart down rather clumsily. Looking up, he saw them: four of them strung out along the window-space, the one nearest the door holding a hat out to passers-by and jiggling it up and down encouragingly. A large piece of cardboard was propped up on the low sill next to the guy, whose head and shoulders leaned against the glass directly in front of the trays of chops.

Jack finished some work with a cleaver, then wiped his hands on the clotted front of his apron and went out to them. 'All right,' he said heavily, 'what's your game then?'

Martin, who was the nearest the door and thus nearest to Jack, backed off a couple of paces. 'Collecting,' he said defensively. 'Penny for the guy.'

'Why do you have to do it here, for God's sake?'

Martin shrugged. 'It's the best place.'

'Is it? Well, I don't want you here. Go on home and take that bloody thing with you.' He flapped a hand at the guy as if it were diseased, then went back into the shop. Martin followed him in.

'I don't think you can stop us,' he said. 'I think we've got every right.' The term seemed inexact, somehow, but it served. 'Every right.' Then he remembered something else: 'Lots of people collect just there. Everyone.' The other children watched him through the window, admiring his stand, but unwilling to add their voices to the argument.

Jack Thompson looked down at the boy and felt something very akin to real hatred. In his boyhood days, there was no questioning an adult. Legalities and rights didn't come into it. Any grown-up outranked any child; you did as you were told; adults were frightening for their knowledge of what you could or couldn't do and omnipotent in enforcing the rules. ' . . . And we're not doing it for ourselves,' Martin went on, 'we're collecting for the orphange.'

Having delivered his *pièce de résistance*, he fell silent. For a moment, they stared at each other, the boy defiant, the man purple with anger. Then Martin went back outside. 'He can't stop us,' he announced to the others, 'we've got every right'; and he shook the brightly-striped ski-hat at passers-by, feeling the coins toss and drop.

On Tuesday, Julian took his turn in the cart. Ben, Tricia and Paul towed it through the streets with Martin in front, collecting as they travelled. At precisely four o'clock they arrived outside Thompson's the Butcher's. Jack Thompson leaned on his knuckles and hung his head between his stiffly extended arms; his fingers whitened against the watery red slick on the chopping board; then he threw down the paring knife he had been using and went out into the street.

'I thought I told you!'

Martin chose to ignore him. Thompson prodded him none too gently with a meaty forefinger, throwing the boy slightly off-balance. 'Answer me when I speak to you, boy. Who do you think you are?'

'We're just collecting for the orphanage,' Martin said without looking at him. 'We're not hurting anything.'

'I thought I told you yesterday. I don't want you outside my shop. Go home . . . ' As he said this, Jack walked over to the cart and kicked it, catching the lower slats with the sole of his shoe; the guy bounced and a hand shot out of the straw cuff, palm-down and pointing at the ground to steady the cart if it went all the way over. Thompson saw none of this. He was back prodding Martin. 'Go home and take that thing with you.'

'Come on, Martin,' Tricia was pulling at his sleeve. 'Come on.' She looked at Thompson warily.

'No,' Martin said. He didn't try to argue any further. Just 'No'. Thompson looked wildly up and down the High Street as if seeking reinforcements. It occurred to Martin that the man might be embarrassed and that seemed a point in the children's favour. The butcher's jaw was rigid with muscle, his face flushed. He spoke through white, inturned lips, the back of one hand rapping on the window as if he were asking to be let in. 'Go away from here. Go away now. You've no right.'

Martin looked at the erratic, flapping hand, then up at the man's face. 'We've got every right,' he said and turned away, jingling his hat at the shoppers.

Tricia looked worried. 'I'm not sure,' she said. 'That man Thompson was incredibly angry yesterday.' She had the trousers and waistcoat on, but had paused for thought before getting into the jacket, the hat and the mask. Tricia felt that the fun had gone out of the enterprise; going back to stand outside Thompson's was a bit like going to the dentist. She hated rows; and the man scared her a bit.

Martin held the jacket out behind her so that she could shrug into it carefully, not displacing any straw. 'It's perfectly all right,' he assured her. 'I told you: I asked my father. I told him what had happened. He said we're perfectly within our rights. In fact, if there's any more trouble, he's going to come down and tackle Thompson about it.'

'But why don't we just go somewhere else?'

'It's the best place,' Martin answered crossly. His annoyance lay chiefly in the fact that, yes, they could have gone somewhere else but, by now, the thing had become a matter of principle for him. He had begun to hate Jack Thompson just a little; hate him for his unreasonableness, for his certainty that he could bully the children into doing something they didn't have to. Other collectors stood there: why shouldn't he? It was one of the points his father had made the previous evening. 'Damn the man,' he had turned to Martin's mother, seeking support and finding it. 'Damn him. Just because they're kids.' Then to Martin: 'Did you tell him it was for the orphanage?'

'Yes. That was *before* he kicked the cart.'

'Look, if there's any trouble tomorrow, come straight home and let me know. I'll go and see him. God! It makes me cross — ' he turned again to his wife, 'just because they're kids; that's all.'

Tricia bounced along in the cart trying to let her limbs jounce to the bumps, swaying, resting her head on her shoulder, letting her heels knock against the rough slats. Oddly, she felt more secure in the cart than she would have simply standing by. If the butcher came out to them again, got cross with them again, she could hide behind the other face of her mask and beneath an anonymous inertness. She admired the way Martin stood up to Mr Thompson and she believed Martin's father when he said that they were doing nothing wrong, but it embarrassed her to stand in the street and be shouted at by an adult; it made her very aware of her status as a child, of the separateness of her world.

When they reached the shop and started collecting, their backs firmly towards the white trays and red meat and the pasty fat of carcasses, Jack Thompson was genuinely surprised to see them. He was sure that his tongue-lashing the day before would have discouraged them. Sure, they had stayed on after he had harangued them — that was simple defiance and a desire to save face. But he hadn't for a moment imagined that they would return. The surprise evaporated and loathing poured in to fill the space. The intensity of what he felt was in part due to humiliation: it

15

was as if he had never spoken, or as if he had spoken and they hadn't heard.

These children made him feel powerless and frustrated and faintly silly. They darkened his life. More than that, though, his loathing found specific targets in the children themselves: the boy with the jingling hat, his arrogance and sureness of his case; the smaller boy who had come with them on the second day, the way his hair fell into a sharp cow's lick; the girl who had been with them yesterday, her moony, sullen look when he had yelled at them; and the backs of their necks, presented to him with skinny indifference.

He did nothing. He felt that to try to send them off again, and fail again, was more than he could bear. But as the afternoon wore on, his hatred grew. Every now and then, his eyes would be drawn to the window; and soon — even when he wasn't looking — he could see the row of backs, of thin necks; could see the slumped figure of the guy and the handles of the cart leaning against his window. He could sense the customers peering between the children, being approached by the boy with the hat as he asked them for money and finally turning away in irritation. They filled his mind, distracting him so that he twice sliced into a finger with the paring knife. He tried not looking at them for ten minutes at a time, but they never left him. Then, turning to replace a ham on its stand, he glanced up and they had gone. The hatred, though, was still there. In his mind's eye, he still saw them ranged along the shopfront. They wouldn't leave him.

'Don't be silly,' Martin said, 'he gave up. He knows he can't stop us. Today and tomorrow still to go and we've already got eight pounds. I bet we get to fifteen!'

'He looks at us through the window, though.' Tricia gave a tiny shiver. 'He frightens me a bit.' She looked back to where, a few paces behind, the others were lugging the hand-cart. The guy's porcine, plastic face stared up at the sky. 'Perhaps we oughtn't to stand there again, Martin?'

'It's the best place,' he retorted stubbornly. 'I don't care about old Thompson. My father will sort him out if he tries it on again.'

As they approached the shop, Martin quickened his pace slightly as if to underline his determination. Before the others were quite in position, he was standing in his usual place, close to the door, and holding out the hat.

Jack Thompson saw them arrive, saw the cart wheeled into position, saw them line up. He had known they would come; and he knew what he was going to do. Put a stop to it. He had decided, the previous evening, that he would put a stop to it as soon as they showed up.

He picked up the paring knife, rounded the counter and walked out into the street. He didn't say a word to them or look at them. He walked up to the cart, stooped, grabbed the guy by its shabby, straw-spattered lapels and slashed and slashed and slashed. Destroy their wretched guy: that's what he would do. Hack its stupid, straw-stuffed head off and throw it away. That ought to make his point.

The children stood rooted to the spot, unable to speak. Then as the blood squirted in a thick, brilliant loop over Thompson's arm, over the paving-stones, over the thin, razor-sharp blade of the knife — as Thompson started back, bellowing with shock and disbelief — Tricia began to scream. She screamed and swayed as if she might pass out; then there was no sound at all except the choking, retching sound that came from behind the guy's mask as the blood pumped in little gushes over the straw cuffs that flailed at its throat. It was Wednesday; it was Ben's turn in the cart.

The Bargain

'This can't be right, can it?'

'What can't be?'

'Just here, look – ' Paul Bennett passed the folded newspaper across the table, his forefinger marking an item in the small ads. He tapped the place to make sure that the other man would find it.

'What, the Jag?' Harry Morris asked him.

'Yes. Just read it.'

Harry muttered his way through the advertisement. 'Jaguar XJS . . . V-reg . . . twenty-two thousand miles, not bad that . . . good repair . . . one owner . . . ' He stopped and looked up at his friend. 'Ten pounds, or near offer? You're joking. It's a misprint; someone's left a few noughts off, mate.'

'That's what I thought.'

'Of course it's a bloody misprint. You didn't really stop to wonder whether some loony might be getting rid of a V-registration Jaguar for a tenner, did you?'

'No, not really.'

'What do you mean, *not really?* I know there are some barmy types about, but they tend not to be the owners of Jaguar cars. I'll bet the poor so-and-so gets a lot of interest, though,' Harry laughed. 'He'll probably have to take his phone off the hook for a week.'

'I don't know,' remarked Paul. 'If we've twigged that it's a printing error, then so will anyone else reading it.' He took the paper back and read the advert again. 'You don't suppose . . . '

'Paul, don't be silly. Honestly. It's a mistake; or a practical joke, perhaps.'

'I just wondered . . . There might be a *reason* for it — I don't know what, it could be anything. Suppose it was being done for a bet: someone saying that he could advertise his car for ten quid and no one would believe it. Then he wins the bet if no one tries to buy the car, but has to sell the car if someone *does* offer him the money.'

'Very far-fetched, kid. You're dreaming again. I know you want a Jag very badly, but the world just isn't like that. There's a very promising-looking Mini in the next column.'

'I could try ringing this number . . . '

'You could, yes. Why don't you? It'll be a complete waste of time, but on the way back you could bring over two more cups of coffee and one of those poisonous sausage rolls that Gladys has had under glass for a decade or so. Go on. I shall be fascinated to hear what the poor, benighted bugger on the other end of the line has to say.'

Paul went to the café counter, ordering the coffees before making his way over to the telephone. His call was answered after no more than a couple of rings. A woman's voice said, 'Jennifer Eames . . . Hullo?'

Paul wasn't at all sure how to begin. Eventually, after she had said 'Hullo' twice more, he said, 'I'm phoning about the ad in the local paper — the Jag — Jaguar; it's advertised for sale.'

'Oh, yes.' He waited for her to say something about the error, but she simply paused, waiting for him to continue.

'Is it . . . I mean, has it gone?'

'No, as a matter of fact, it hasn't. To tell you the truth,

19

you're the first caller.'

'An XJS, V-registration?'

'That's right.'

'Ten pounds? A tenner?'

'That's right.'

'Well — ' He didn't know what to think. 'Perhaps you could tell me . . . what's wrong with it?'

'Nothing, so far as I know. It was serviced not so long ago; it's running perfectly well; it's not . . . ' She paused as if uncertain of the correct terminology to employ. ' . . . *unsound* in any way.'

'It hasn't been in an accident, or anything of that sort?'

'Oh, good gracious no. Nothing like that, I promise you.'

'And you've got all the papers, proof of ownership and so on?'

'Sorry?' There was a crispness in the well-bred voice at this, the merest suggestion of outrage — or was it querulousness?

'It's just . . . I'm sorry; you have got proof of ownership?'

'Of course.'

He knew he should ask her. He knew there had to be a reason; something had to be wrong. But he couldn't — just couldn't — bring himself to face the disillusionment. Not right then. Not yet. As long as he didn't ask, it would go on being true.

'Well, Mr . . . ah . . . '

'Bennett.'

'Mr Bennett, would you like to come and see the car, or not?'

'I could come over now, if you're going to be in,' he said hurriedly. 'Is that convenient?'

'Perfectly,' she said. 'The house is called "Weirfield". It's in Manor Drive, at the far end. Do you know where I mean?'

'Yes. I'll be there in about half an hour. Is that O.K.?'

'I'll be here,' said the woman. 'See you shortly, Mr Bennett.'

20

He went back to the table where Harry was leafing aimlessly through the paper. As Paul sat down, he looked up and smiled knowingly. 'Joke or printer's error? And you've forgotten the coffees and the lethal sausage roll.'

'It's right.'

Harry raised his head slowly. 'You what?'

'It's for sale for ten quid. V-reg, hasn't been in a prang, good running order, she said, and they're asking ten pounds.'

'Joke,' Harry insisted, 'or printer's error?'

'Christ, you don't think I'd torture myself by trying to con you about something as close to my heart as this, do you?' There was something in Paul's voice that made Harry pay attention. 'It's absolutely true. No joke, no mistake. I asked her twice.'

'Then it's a more complicated joke than I suspected at first.'

'I don't know so much, Harry. She didn't sound like a person who would mess about like that. She was a bit posh, you know, sounded very upper-middle; and the house is in Manor Drive.'

'Certainly the place for a Jag,' Harry said. 'There are no houses up there that would go for less than a hundred thousand.'

'Well,' Paul spread his hands and shrugged. 'What have I got to lose?' Behind the casualness was a thread of urgency. 'Like I said earlier; there might be a reason — some explanation. I'm going to go over there. Do you want to come?'

'I don't think so.' Harry shook his head. 'I'll just wait for you here. I'm not sure I could stand to watch you break down when you realize the whole thing's a hoax. You go.'

'She said mine was the first inquiry,' said Paul, as if to encourage his friend to join him.

'I'll bet it was. The first and only unless I'm mistaken. Look, go on. You'll worry about it until you're old and grey otherwise. I'll wait here. Try not to be hysterical in public when you get back.' He grinned. 'Go on. If you come back with a ten-quid Jag, I'll buy the next round of what they laughingly refer to as coffee in this caff.'

Paul caught a bus that took him to the top of Manor Drive. 'Weirfield' was an imposing place: half-a-dozen bedrooms at least, he thought, and worth a deal more than Harry's figure of a hundred thousand. The long driveway was flanked by more than half an acre of lawns and shrubbery; leaves shed by the enormous chestnut tree on the right-hand lawn had been raked into a series of neat mounds.

A woman opened the door to his knock. The same woman; the same well-modulated, soft voice; attractive, with a slender figure, good, strong features and clear blue eyes. Thirtyish, he thought, maybe thirty-five. She pushed back a heavy lock of corn-coloured hair and regarded him. 'Mr Bennett?'

'Yes. About the car.'

'Yes. It's this way.'

She half-closed the front door and brushed past him, leading the way to a double garage at the side of the house. The doors were open. Inside were two cars: a Lancia and a Jaguar XJS, its racing green immaculate, its bodywork undented, its upholstery looking like new.

She stood nearby while he examined it, checking under the bonnet, scrambling underneath to inspect the chassis, scrutinizing the tyres and the interior and, finally, switching on the engine to let it tick over.

'Would you like to road test it, perhaps? We could go for a short drive. Not too long — I've got an appointment in twenty minutes.'

He didn't need to take it on the road. He could see perfectly well that the car would have been a bargain at three hundred times the price, or more. Taking a deep breath, almost flinching at the expectation of something disastrous in the offing, he removed two five-pound notes from his wallet.

'This is right, is it?' he asked. 'If I give you these, then the car's mine. Ten pounds.' He pointed at the Jag. 'For this.'

'Correct, Mr Bennett. Thank you.' She twitched the bank-notes out of his fingers, then folded them over a couple of times, running the nails of her thumb and first finger down the crease. 'The documents that you asked about are in the glove-compartment. Oh,' she fished in a pocket, 'and here's a receipt for the ten pounds.' She smiled. 'I anticipated you.'

He took the piece of paper she offered to him and examined it. Then he looked at her for a second or two, before saying: 'You had better tell my why, don't you think? This car − for ten quid. I had better know why.'

'I wondered when you'd ask. Don't worry, Mr Bennett,' she pushed the money into her back pocket, 'it's all perfectly legal and free of snags. But I'll tell you. Yes, I'd better tell you, I imagine. You might see the funny side of it. You see, my husband left me a couple of weeks ago; ran off with someone he'd been having an affair with. Left me high and dry − a note on the mantelpiece, the coward's way, don't you agree, and not very original.' Her voice was still calm, still soft. 'He sent me a letter a few days ago, asking me to have his clothes and whatnot sent to his office. He also asked me to sell his car and send the proceeds to him.' She took the two five-pound notes from her pocket and looked at them. She smiled. 'He won't get many candle-lit suppers out of this, will he?'

Predictions

She was standing at a bus-stop on a long, straight stretch of country road, her back turned to a strong, warm wind that bore tracers of rain like flails — her back turned so that her black mackintosh was moulded to her body and flew, as her heavy, dark-blonde hair flew, in the wake of the gusting wind. The spread of beech boughs that overhung the road rolled and furled, shedding big, shimmering globes of water that floated through the thinner drift, elongating as the wind carried them, then splattering brief silver on the dark asphalt.

Her hands were thrust into her mac pockets, her shoulders hunched against the blow. At each sound of an engine, she turned her head to see if it was the bus arriving. Her hair trailed across her face and fluttered like a pennant; she tilted her head to clear it from her eyes. In the strange, flexing light — sharp gunmetal beams funnelling up the road between the intense, shifting green of the beeches — the beautiful, eerie violet of those eyes seemed preternaturally bright.

As soon as Lawrence Porter saw her, he changed down a gear and began to slow the car in order to pick her up. He had several reasons for doing this: she looked as though she might be pretty; the weather was, he thought, really foul; so far as he knew, there wasn't a bus due along that road for at least another fifteen minutes; and – after all – there was a war on and people should help each other out, he believed, as best they could.

When he drew up alongside the bus-stop, he expected that she would turn towards the car. She didn't. She continued to huddle against the wind. He tapped the horn to attract her attention and she looked round as if noticing him for the first time, although he knew that she had seen him coming along the road: she had turned as she heard the car. That was when he had thought she might be pretty, her face half-hidden by the swathe of tawny hair; that was when he had begun to slow down and steer in towards the kerb. She looked over towards him, but she didn't move. He leaned across to the passenger's side, wound the window down and poked his head out, ignoring the spray of wind-blown rainwater.

'I'm going into Oxford,' he called. 'Can I offer you a lift?'

For another three or four seconds, she continued to stand there, gazing at him and saying nothing. Then she walked over to the car and got in.

'Pretty wet out there,' he said as they moved off. 'You *are* going to Oxford?'

'Yes I am.' Her voice was soft and light and for the first time, she smiled. 'It's very kind of you. I'm grateful.'

'Not at all,' Lawrence smiled back. 'Glad to be of help.'

A gust of wind batted the car sideways. The noise of it, together with the drumming of rain on the roof and the rowdiness of the little Austin Seven, made it necessary to shout to be heard.

'I'm a vet,' Lawrence told the girl.

'Sorry?' She leaned slightly towards him as if to catch his words.

'A vet.'

'Ah, yes.'

25

'That's why I get the petrol. Mercy dashes to cows in calf and horses with festering hooves: that sort of thing. Shouldn't use it for joy-riding really, but the weather looked so foul.' He paused, but she made no answer. He glanced towards her, then quickly back again. She really was very pretty, he hadn't been mistaken about that; and he had noticed that the fingers of her ungloved hands were ringless. Maybe, he thought, she would accept an invitation to dinner. He tried to keep the conversation going – or, rather, to get it started.

'Live in Oxford, do you?'

'Yes,' was all she gave him.

'Lovely city; lovely. I wish I'd been there in my student days, but it wasn't to be. Not bright enough, I suppose. Went to Bristol. Parents wanted me to be a doctor, but I'd always been fonder of animals than people . . . excepting some people of course,' he added this last rather daringly. 'What do you do?'

When he got no reply, he looked across at her again. She was staring fixedly at the metronomic movement of the windscreen-wiper, at the way the semi-circular beading of rainwater appeared to be drawn by the tip of the blade, then started to form droplets and run down the glass only to be re-drawn as the blade passed back. Her violet eyes were jewelled and if Lawrence had been able to look at her for as long as he would have liked, he would have noticed that the reflection of water from the screen left them sometimes spangled with colour, sometimes shuttered by white light.

'What do you do?' He raised his voice against the engine's row.

She smiled at him – almost indulgently it seemed, as though he were a persistent child. 'You'll find it strange.' Her soft voice carried perfectly above the din.

'Oh surely not? I say, you're not a German spy are you – checking on the deployment of vets in the Home Counties so that Hitler's menagerie of generals can be checked for

26

rabies and ear-canker after the invasion?'

She didn't laugh at his weak joke, but the smile stayed. 'I'm a fortune-teller,' she said.

'Good Lord.'

'I said you'd find it odd.'

'Not at all. Well . . . a little, perhaps. I wasn't expecting it. You mean "Madame Rosa, the Gypsy Palmist" — booths at the fair, seaside, that sort of thing? Cross my palm with silver, tall dark men in teacups and so on?'

'More or less. Except that people come to me by appointment and I don't read palms or tea-leaves.'

'Oh, look, I'm sorry. I wasn't trying to make fun, you know.'

'It's all right.'

'No, really,' he insisted. 'It's very interesting.' The conversation wasn't going at all in the direction he had hoped. How could he invite her out if she thought he was laughing at her? He was discountenanced, a little mystified and, if anything, more attracted to her than before — taken aback by what she had said, but not put off. He offered a second, more subtle, apology by asking her what she meant: what did a fortune-teller *do?*

She gave a tiny sigh and rearranged her legs in the cramped space. 'Fortune-teller isn't the right term really. People call us that, so we sometimes call ourselves that. Especially those who actually go in for fairground tents and the like. Some do, even the most talented. Some are charlatans, of course; fakes. Many have a real gift. Fortune-tellers — it's one of those names that people in a specialized field use to describe themselves because they feel a little self-defensive. And they feel self-defensive because the term is wrongly — disparagingly — used by others. Do you see?'

'I think so.' He *did* think so, but it didn't answer his question, so he asked it again.

'Nothing really. I mean, no props or anything. I used to,

when I thought people really needed crystal balls and Tarot cards and so on, but I became rather tired of that sort of client. They wanted to hear only good things, but they didn't believe them anyway. It's a sort of parlour game for such people; they tend to go in for after-dinner séances and planchette boards.' The extraordinary eyes regarded him, but seemed not to have the light of mockery in them.

'Yes, I see . . . but you still haven't said how you − how you carry on, if you see what I mean. A client − comes to you . . . what for? And what happens?'

'Fortune-teller doesn't mean anything. I can predict − sometimes; other times not. It depends what the client wants; to find someone who is missing, perhaps. To ask for advice. Or, yes, to see into the future. "Fortune-teller" is wrong; I'm a psychic. I respond to atmospheres, places, things. I gain an understanding of people and events through the power that lies in objects and rooms and so forth. What makes it special, my . . . gift . . . is that sometimes the people aren't actually present and the events haven't happened.'

'What about the beyond? The life beyond. I mean, do you get in touch with those who have passed on? You know: messages from beyond the grave for those still here?'

Her eyes fluttered shut for a moment and her head shook: the merest trace of a gesture. 'The dead are dead. Mediums are almost always crooks.'

'But it must be exciting,' he stopped, realizing how condescending this sounded. 'Your talent, I mean. It must be a great boon.' He had tried to find a word that would put value on what she did − what she was.

'Predicting the winner of the three-thirty at Cheltenham, you mean, or knowing which stocks will fall and which will rise? It doesn't work like that.'

She laughed, then fell silent again. Lawrence couldn't think of anything to add. He drove on through the piling rain, correcting for the car's movement as the wind hit it on open stretches, conscious of the girl's quiet presence in a very particular, oddly palpable way, steering and changing gear and negotiating corners with the exaggerated, almost clumsy carefulness of someone who is being closely observed. She wasn't observing him, however; she was gazing out through the windscreen again, utterly still, as if lulled by the noise of the weather and the clatter of the car.

They travelled for about a mile before she spoke. Her voice was slightly dulled as if she were emerging from a doze. 'Sometimes, in fact, it's anything but a boon. It can be a curse, sometimes.'

Pleased by the fact that she had spoken first, he encouraged her with a quick question. He wanted her to want to tell him about herself. 'Is it? In what way?'

'I don't always want to know what there is to know. I don't always want to tell people what they're asking for.'

'And do you?'

'Usually. Not always.'

'How do you decide?'

'Well, if I have to make a decision at all, it's probably because I'm passing on bad news. It depends on the news and the person. In any case, I'm not always being *asked*, if you follow me. Sometimes I simply know something about a person or a place without having been approached for a prediction. More often than not, it works that way – in unguarded moments rather than when I'm concentrating.'

'But *could* you know the winner of a race that hadn't taken place, for example?'

'I doubt it. More powerful things, more important things; it seems to have to do with them. Oh,' she uttered it as though it were an afterthought, 'I know when the war's going to end. I know that.'

'Good God. How?' He was genuinely startled by her matter-of-fact tone.

'How?'

'How do you know . . . why, I mean. Why did you think of it?'

29

'Oh, somebody asked me and I knew. It just . . . I'd said the date before thinking. I knew it was right.'

'When?'

' . . . will it end?'

'Yes.'

'Next May. The 8th.'

'May 8th, 1945?'

'Yes.'

'Good gracious.' He could think of nothing else to say. She smiled at his evident confusion and allowed another silence to settle. They had reached the outskirts of Oxford, descending a long hill towards Magdalen Bridge; after they had passed Magdalen Tower, she said, 'Thank you. Anywhere near here.'

He drove into Longwall and stopped. 'Will this do?'

'Oh yes,' she turned to him. 'Yes, this is perfect. Thank you again. It was very kind.'

The strangeness of their conversation had diverted him from the business of plotting a strategy for asking her out. He still wanted to do that, but couldn't think of a way; any approach would seem too abrupt. He had hoped for a slow progression, through civilized small-talk, to a nicely-timed invitation to lunch or dinner. As it was, he didn't even know her name, or where she lived, didn't have the slightest notion of whether she already had a young man or was likely to accept an invitation. He could think of nothing appropriate, but wanted to delay her. As she clutched the door-catch, he blurted another question.

'Has your gift told you anything about me?'

He saw her shoulders stiffen; her face was turned away from him and she had swivelled towards the door in order to get out. A stillness came over her — as if she were tensed against movement, or against speech.

'Nothing really, no.' She hadn't looked at him as she spoke. He knew she was telling a lie. He felt a small shock, like being lightly struck, and a momentary dizziness.

'There's something.' The firmness in his voice held her. She leaned back against the seat, but kept her hand on the catch. The violet eyes regarded him unwaveringly. Their colour deepened until its intensity startled him.

She said: 'Someone will die in this car today.'

He felt angry; the small shock became anger but he couldn't rationalize it. 'I see,' he snapped. 'The war will end on May 8th next year and someone will die here in my car today. Is that it?'

'Yes,' she said, very softly. Her voice was laden with regret but her eyes didn't flinch. 'Yes.' And he knew the anger was really fear.

'Is it me?'

'I don't know.'

'Who is it?'

'I don't know.' She opened the door and got out into the rain, then bent down to look in the door. Her hair blew across her face, so she lifted a hand to stroke it back, holding it in place while, from the other temple, it lifted and fluffed in the swirling wind. 'I'm sorry,' she said. Then she walked back along the pavement and turned the corner.

He did some shopping and picked up a few items from the dispensary in Broad Street, then dumped his purchases in the car before going to the Lamb and Flag. It was his Oxford local; his pint was drawn before he had lodged himself at the bar. He was still thinking about the girl, regretting his sharpness with her and regretting, too, that he hadn't asked for her name. Mixed with the memory of desire, though, was a feeling of unease. He recalled the look on her face as she had made her prediction; and he reflected that she didn't seem the type to play games or try to scare him.

He finished his beer and pushed his glass across the bar for another. The barmaid hauled on the pump. 'When do you think the war will end, Beryl?'

'Soon, I hope.' She put the glass down at his elbow and

31

swept up the coppers he had laid on the bar.

'If you had to guess, though. If you were making a prediction.'

'Well, I don't know, Mr Porter. That's for the politicians, isn't it? Perhaps Mr Churchill knows — or Hitler. You could try sending him a telegraph.'

'It's just that somebody told me today . . . ' He didn't complete the remark and she waited.

'Told you what?'

'It doesn't matter.' He took a swallow of beer. For some reason he suddenly felt superstitiously cautious about repeating the prediction: as he used to feel as a child, when saying you wanted something might somehow lessen the chance of getting it. 'It doesn't matter.' He put the glass down and glanced over towards the window. 'Filthy weather.' Beryl was easily diverted; she chatted on about the iniquities of the English climate while Lawrence's mind roamed back to the girl. There had seemed to be a weight of sadness in her, a solemnity, as if she lived beyond the possibility of gaiety or unalloyed delight, but could detect it in others and was depressed by her lack of talent for it. She lived, he reasoned, with some burden; and the more that understanding was borne in on him, the surer he became that she had told him the truth — or, at least, the truth of her vision.

'Is it me?'

'I don't know.'

'Who is it?'

'I don't know.'

That last exchange ran in his mind, making him shudder. *'Is it me?'*

'Lawrence?' He turned to the voice. 'Lawrence, hullo. I thought it was you.'

'Hullo, Gordon. Have a drink.'

'I will. A whisky, thank you.' Gordon Archer sat down and rubbed his hands, anticipating the drink. He owned one of the largest farms in the district and could be counted among Lawrence's most regular clients. The whisky arrived and Gordon offered a toast, 'Here's to land-girls', drinking it off at one go. Lawrence waved at Beryl for another.

'How's Fernyhill Major?'

'A bad-tempered sod, and getting worse,' laughed Gordon. 'Still got the bruises?'

Fernyhill Major was a Hereford bull with homicidal tendencies. Lawrence had been to the farm to treat the animal a month previously when the Major had tried a right hook which missed, a left hook which had torn a pocket from Lawrence's overalls, and then had pinned him to the stall with a shoulder as he had moved to escape.

'Yes I have − together with a strong sense of resentment. I'd be glad to have the first prime steak off that creature when the time comes.'

They talked animals and what ails them over a couple more drinks, until Lawrence looked at his watch and announced that he ought to be getting back.

'OK.' Gordon consulted his own watch. 'Are you going back directly? Maybe you could drop me at the end of the lane, if you've got the car, that is.'

'I could, yes. I have got it. I could drop you at the farm in fact; it's not much of a diversion and the weather's so bad.' He said the words quickly, reflexively, and drank the rest of his beer, and listened to Gordon telling him that he was being very decent and, well, if it wouldn't put him to too much trouble . . . and he knew, at the back of his mind, why he had agreed to give the lift but hadn't offered it; why he had not mentioned the girl; and heard his voice asking, '*Is it me?*'

As they left Oxford, Lawrence was very conscious that he was driving with the kind of exaggerated concentration that learners have, before de-clutching and changing gear and steering become second nature. Gordon's conversation was an annoyance to him. He couldn't listen and answer and handle the car. At first he felt ridiculous, then angry; and the anger steadied him, so that his control became surer and soon he was back in the way of driving properly again: responding automatically, until that confidence that drivers usually have and passengers often lack settled on him and he relaxed. By the time they had reached the stretch where he had picked up the girl, he had almost completely forgotten to feel anxious. She might well have felt the truth of what she had told him; that didn't mean, though, that it would *become* the truth. No, the truth was this uneventful drive, the little car pottering through the rain towards home. The truth was dropping Gordon at the farm, being offered a cup of tea before setting off again. The truth was getting home and preparing for the early-evening surgery.

He wondered whether he would ever meet the girl again. He hoped he would. He even devised a line for the occasion: 'Hullo, I didn't die and I wonder if you'd like to celebrate the fact with me over dinner.' An amused, gentle chiding coupled with an invitation she could scarcely decline, given the circumstances. He thought about her; and as her face took form in his mind's eye, so he saw her — or thought he saw her — in the flesh, standing at the bus-stop where she had been earlier in the day, her face turned from the rain, her hair awry in the wind.

He looked at her, not knowing what to think or what to do. His senses, his reactions, narrowed to her presence as they would to a figure spotlit in a darkened auditorium. A roar built in his skull, as if the wind had entered his head to funnel through caverns in his brain and he was hardly aware of Gordon's shout of warning, or the jolt and lurch when the car left the road and ploughed down the roadside bank into the trees. There was something like an explosion, a distant explosion, as the windscreen went and the branch came into the car like a pile-driver. It tore Gordon Archer's face almost completely away, leaving his head spiked on its ragged end, skewered and shredded and featureless.

34

Lawrence looked at it through the haze of blood that seemed to be covering his eyes. He looked away. He wasn't badly hurt. They took glass from his forehead and scalp and treated him for shock and mild concussion, keeping him in hospital overnight for observation. He lay in the penumbral gloom of the ward, staring at the half-globe of the night-light opposite his bed. He knew why he had given Gordon the lift. He knew why. He knew why he was glad to have been able to take a passenger. *'Is it me?'* he heard himself ask. *'Is it me? Is it me?'* He let the glowing lamp print on his retinas. The pain above his eyes ebbed and flowed. He knew when the war would end.

A Dash for Freedom

'We're excited, aren't we Tweetie? Mummy's excited and Tweetie's excited. It's going to be an exciting day.' The budgerigar sat on Mrs Potter's finger and riffled its wing feathers. An impartial observer would have been obliged to state, if asked, that Tweetie showed few signs of excitement – or, indeed, of any other strong emotion. It is true, though, that the moods of budgerigars are not easily discerned. By and large, they appear to wear an expression of mild truculence – something, perhaps, to do with the curve of their beaks. Mrs Potter was in no doubt, however.

'You *are* excited, aren't you?' she chuckled as the bird flew up on to her shoulder. 'Oh, yes. So excited. Just like Mummy.'

The reason for the excitement, whether or not Tweetie shared it, was that Mrs Potter was to have new carpets that day. Fitted carpets. Proper carpets. The carpets she had been saving for during the past two years or so. Slowly but surely, over the years since her husband's death, Mrs Potter had been paying to have her small terraced house redecorated. Arthur had always done it before: the papering and painting, the odd jobs that needed attending to. They had always promised themselves a proper, fitted carpet; it seemed an enormous luxury; but the money had been diverted to other, more essential things. Now, there was just enough.

'What a pity', Mrs Potter said to the bird, 'that Daddy won't be here to enjoy the new carpets. What a pity.' Tweetie had outlived Mr Potter, a fact that Mr Potter might well have found undignified; and Mrs Potter, in her quieter moments, was put to wondering whether she would prefer to die before the bird, thereby being assured of companionship for the rest of her life, or be the last to go so that she wouldn't have to worry (and she did worry) about what would happen to Tweetie after her death. Tweetie's welfare gave Mrs Potter great concern.

It would have been difficult to say whether he felt quite the same way about her, but there was no doubt that, since Mr Potter had 'fallen asleep' — the legend on his gravestone asserted it — Tweetie had become an increasingly important part of Mrs Potter's life. Her monologues, thanks to Tweetie, became conversations. Her questions could be answered on Tweetie's behalf. There was someone to come home to after her little expeditions to the shops. There was someone to be looked after and fed and made comfortable.

'Now,' said Mrs Potter, getting up from her chair, 'you have your little fly, while Mummy gets your surprise.' She went into the kitchen and returned with a sheet of sandpaper and some cuttlefish. 'Tweetie's going to have a new carpet, just like Mummy. And something tasty to peck at.' While she cleaned the cage out, the budgie ambled round the room, hopping from floor to sideboard, back to the floor and from there on to the back of a dining-chair. Then he flew through the doorway into the hall and up the stairs. Mrs Potter paused to think; then she nodded to herself. Yes, she had remembered to shut all the upstairs windows. There had been an occasion not long ago when she had almost lost Tweetie for good. He had flown upstairs and found a fanlight open: a window, quite literally, on a world that lay beyond Tweetie's wildest imaginings. It may have been that the variety and profusion of it all stunted his ambition, though, for he contented himself with perching on a telegraph wire no more than a short glide from the house until a fireman on a turntable ladder managed to coax him back into his cage. Ever since that awful day, Mrs Potter had been careful to ensure that all windows were firmly latched before letting Tweetie flutter freely about the house.

When the cage was ready, spruce and tempting with its new floor-covering and the fresh slab of cuttlefish wedged between the bars, she recovered Tweetie from the top of her wardrobe and closed the cage door behind him. As she did so, the doorbell chimed.

'That'll be the carpet men, Tweets,' she informed the bird, wrestling with the stiff hook on the bars of the cage. 'How exciting!' She let them in, clucking with delight over the beautiful mustard-coloured carpet they were carrying between them. It looked more impressive than ever: three enormous rolls of it; much grander than the rug-sized piece she had picked out at the carpet showroom.

'The best thing for you to do', one of the men informed her after she had shown them the rooms in which the carpet was to be laid, 'would be to take yourself off somewhere while we get down to it. We'll be moving your furniture about, carting it from room to room and so on. Better if you came back when it's finished.'

She agreed. She didn't want to see the disruption, the cuts of carpet rucked and thrown down to wait their turn; didn't want to see the mechanics of it. She would much prefer to go out now and come back when it was all perfect: all done.

'It won't take that long,' the man told her. 'Come back at about half-past three. Treat yourself to some lunch in a caff, love.'

And that was exactly what she did. A potter about the shops, a trip to the supermarket for a few eggs, some cereal and a packet of budgie seed, and then on to Granny's Pantry, the nicest of the nearby restaurants, for a poached egg. After that, she went to the library for a while. It wasn't a place she visited often, she and Tweetie both preferred the television; but from time to time she would call in to get something for those nights when she couldn't manage to fall asleep within a few minutes of getting in to bed. She didn't much like the library. Too many old folk sat around there, trying to find company, or strike up a conversation. They went there, she knew, for want of anywhere else to go − and she was sorry for them. But she didn't want to feel a part of that wanton loneliness; it didn't affect her because she − unlike the poor souls who sometimes journeyed through rain or snow just to be near another human being − had all she needed: her little house, her telly, Tweetie; and after today, of course, her brand-new fitted carpets.

The men had just finished putting the furniture back when she got home. The carpets looked glorious − simply glorious, she thought. She was so pleased that she tried to give the men a tip, but they refused, gently, somewhat embarrassed, telling her that there were others richer than she who could tip if they liked, but no one would catch them taking tips from an OAP.

After they had gone, she stood in the middle of her sitting-room and turned round slowly. Then she turned back the other way. 'Oh, Tweetie,' she said. *'Isn't* it splendid?' The mustard-colour was exactly right, exactly how she had pictured it, a perfect match for the wallpaper and the curtains, blending tastefully with the upholstery and cushions. 'Oh, Tweetie.' She turned round once again. 'It does look *splendid.'*

On her fourth twirl of inspection, she took in the budgerigar's cage. Her gaze had moved on before her brain registered what she had seen. The door was slightly open and the cage was empty. She went over, heart in mouth. It had happened before. The hook was stiff and didn't always catch in its loop properly. Her attention had been taken that morning by the arrival of the carpet-layers and she must have neglected to fasten it securely. She thought back. All the windows had been closed, she knew that; but perhaps the workmen had opened one — to let the dust out, or to waft away the smoke from their cigarettes; perhaps they had left the front door open at some stage.

She walked to the door that led into the hallway and pulled it towards her. It stuck on some tiny undulation in the carpet. She yanked at it, but it wouldn't open more than a few inches.

'Blast them!' she said, fear provoking an uncharacteristic anger. 'First they let Tweetie out, then they leave lumps in my carpet.' She pushed the door closed and examined the obstruction: a blip some six inches from the door's edge. She tried again, but the door wouldn't pass over it.

'Tweetie!' she called, peering through the crack between door and frame to look up the stairway. 'Tweetie!' She tugged at the door once more, then, in panic and anger, stamped her foot on the lump in the carpet, trying to flatten it. It worked. The door moved a little further, almost clearing the tuck, so she stamped again, harder, then went over to the bookshelf and got down Arthur's big carpentry manual. Kneeling down by the door, she slammed the book down as hard as she could on the lump: five times, six, seven. When she tried it, the door cleared the carpet easily. She ran up the stairs and into the bedrooms, checking windows and calling, 'Tweetie, Tweetie. Where are you, Tweets? Come to Mummy.'

Downstairs, a small dab of red appeared against the carpet's mustard, spreading, until it was about the size of an egg.

Heads You Lose

In the space of six months or so, Jennie Curtis had become
a very skilful liar. She lied with the kind of ease that practice
brings; she lied with a casualness born of devotion; and she
hadn't yet learned to regret lying, or be afraid of it, or
ashamed. There are those who lie because it amuses them,
and those who lie from habit. Others lie from necessity and
they are the ones whose lies come most easily.

Jennie lied to her parents, who believed her lies, and to
her friends, who believed her most of the time, and to
herself, but that was a different kind of lie and she was only
vaguely aware of the fact that she was telling it. Peter was
telling lies of necessity, too. He was lying to his wife. The
combination of those two sets of lies made it possible for
Peter and Jennie to meet on two evenings in each week to
make love and tell each other what both believed to be the
truth: that they were in love, that nothing like this had ever
happened to either of them and that – finally – they would
be together . . . just as soon as Peter was able to find the
right moment to tell his wife that he was sorry but these
things happened, he had found someone he *really* loved,
and, of course, he would provide for the kids and continue
to pay off the mortgage. When he did that – when the right

moment arrived — Jennie would confess to her parents and everyone could stop lying.

At first, the lies had been oddly exciting. After three or four months, though, the pattern of deception and the exhilaration of escape had palled for Jennie; and it occurred to her that Peter was finding it difficult to make the break. She didn't reject the idea, she found excuses for it while continuing to believe that it was simply a matter of time and the summoning of enough courage to face the moment. The alternative — that he was lying to her — was too painful to contemplate. So while he bided his time, they would continue to meet on Tuesdays and Thursdays (never weekends, of course), have dinner in some nearby town where neither was likely to be recognized and make love in the back seat of his car, in the dark, in a country lane on the way home, before he dropped her three streets away from her house.

Jennie left the house, as usual, at seven-thirty. It took exactly fifteen minutes to walk to the station; and at seven-forty-five Peter's red company Cortina arrived at the approach to the station forecourt. She climbed in, quickly, since this was the riskiest part of their meeting, and huddled down in the passenger-seat until they were clear of the outskirts.

'Chinese, Indian, Greek or Italian?' She knew which restaurants he was thinking of.

'Indian?'

'O.K.'

'I had Greek for lunch.'

'O.K.' He laughed. 'I think you can probably come up now.'

She surfaced and kissed him energetically while he tried to take a bend. 'I know what you mean,' he assured her, 'but we'll have to eat first. Light evenings . . . '

'I wish . . . '

'I promise,' he cut her off, ' — we'll be together soon.'

She opened her mouth to ask how soon 'soon' was; then changed her mind and kissed him again.

The meal was spent, as it almost always was, discussing themselves. As they left, the manager bowed slightly, in a rather quaint way, inclining his head and wishing them good night. They were known in the restaurant — indeed, they were known in all the restaurants they visited. Jennie recalled how it used to please her that they should be recognized as a couple; it meant, somehow, that their relationship was well-founded.

Peter swung the car out on to the main road, then turned off it almost immediately. They almost always went to the same place: a tiny track off a B-road that led to a gate and some pasture. It was obvious that the track was used only when cattle were being herded to or from the farm that lay some half-mile away. Now and then, to their annoyance, they would find the place already occupied by a parked car; Peter would back swiftly and angrily down the track, not angry so much at finding the place taken, as discomfited by evidence that they were one of many couples touring the dark roads looking for somewhere to hurry through a furtive love-making. The track was about ten miles along the minor road and they spent the first five minutes or so of the journey in silence.

'Have you thought any more about our weekend?' The first couple of words clemmed in her throat and she had to cough and repeat them. He didn't reply. 'Peter?'

'Of course I have. I'm working on it.'

'What do you . . . ?'

'It's not easy. I'm dropping hints about wanting to get away on my own; and I've introduced a company training-course for good measure. It has to be done carefully.'

'Why?' The wine she had drunk during dinner had made her a little petulant; she felt secure enough to take a risk.

'Why?' she repeated. 'Tell her and get it over with. I thought you were going to.'

He said nothing; and in the silence, her security evaporated. 'I'm sorry.' She tried to keep the fear out of her voice. 'I just want you to myself for a bit. You know.'

He had things under control again, now, and could afford to inject a quiet fervour into his tone when he answered, 'Don't you think I want it that way?'

She put a hand on his knee and stroked slowly upwards. He said, 'Mmm,' and put his hand over hers, encouraging it, and nursing the silence that seemed to be in his favour. Then, as a way of sealing the conversation with a concession, he said: 'Of course, look, it can't go on like this. I've got a few things to sort out − the house, a lawyer, all that stuff; as soon as that's done . . . ', he shrugged exaggeratedly so that she would notice, ' . . . she gets the bad news.'

They were half-way there. The road was dark and straight and lonely, flanked by tall trees that could be heard but scarcely seen. There were no street-lights, no house lights, just a faint sodium glow on the horizon that marked the position of the town. Peter had the headlights full up and the occasional signpost glowed whitely. Twice they saw something run across the road ahead of them, from one part of the wood to another − foxes taking their chances. On a long, black stretch where the trees bordering the road curved in on each other to make a gloomy tunnel, the car glided to a slow halt. Jennie looked across, surprised. The car stuttered, picked up for a few yards, then freewheeled again.

'For God's sake!'

'What is it?' She still wasn't sure whether it was some capriciousness or a mechanical problem.

He braked, switched off and turned to her. 'You're not going to believe this, but we've run out of petrol.'

'You're kidding?'

44

'It might seem about the least necessary thing for me to have to do, child, but I have run out of petrol.' He looked helplessly at the needle on the gauge, as if it might oblige him by swinging away from the 'E'.

She giggled. 'That's ridiculous. To say nothing of corny. Not to mention unnecessary.'

'I just said that.' There was an edge in his tone and she picked it up and knew perfectly well what it meant. Then she felt a touch of panic on her own account. He wasn't the only one who was likely to have some explaining to do.

'Where are we?' Roughly speaking, she knew. What she meant was what he was thinking: how *far* are we . . . from town, from where we should be, from a filling station? He got out of the car, taking the keys with him, and banged around in the boot until he came up with a plastic jerrycan. 'Have you got a pound note?'

'Yes . . . what . . . ?'

'About four miles down this road,' he explained, 'there's a garage. It's not open all night, but they have one of those pumps where you feed a quid into a slot and the pump discharges about 80p's-worth of petrol. I haven't got a pound note.'

She handed over the money. He sighed deeply and swore. 'It's about four miles,' he repeated. 'I don't suppose I'll get a lift. I'll be as quick as I can.' He looked along the road, through the tunnel of trees. The uppermost branches opened and closed on lighter-coloured planes of night sky as the wind first drew them and then let them swing back into their arch.

'How long do you think you'll be? I could come with you.' The question and suggestion ran into each other, first nervous then distinctly anxious. He understood. 'Just lock yourself into the car; you'll be O.K. I'll probably jog some of the way. You'll be all right.' He really did think he could get to the garage and back faster on his own, that much was true. He could see she was a little scared, maybe more than

45

a little, but he didn't want a question-and-answer session —
prompted by their predicament and the likelihood of hard
questions being asked elsewhere — over eight miles of
country roads. It was troubling enough that he would have
to come up with a convincing excuse when he arrived
home. The obvious one, that he had run out of petrol on the
way back, seemed the least likely to be believed somehow.
It would have been kinder to have taken Jennie with him,
but he wasn't going to and he knew it. 'Just lock the car
doors — you'll be fine.' By way of emphasis he slammed the
driver's door, then peered through the window and smiled.
She smiled back and made a hurrying gesture, then snapped the lock down.

After half an hour or so, she checked her watch. It was
almost 11.30. The average person walks at about four miles
per hour, she reasoned. So walking briskly, he would be
two-thirds of the way there. Jogging, maybe there already.
She drummed up a mental picture of him by the petrol
pump, reading the instructions, flattening out the bank
note and placing it on the metal tray, holding the can under
the nozzle in the light of the garage's all-night neon. Stupidly, she began the same calculation about his pace over
the distance for coming back, muttering it to herself as a
kind of reassurance. 'Walking: four miles per hour; jogging,
say seven miles per hour; jogging half-way, two miles at
four miles per hour, two miles at *Christ what was that?*' She
didn't actually speak the words, but their essence was in the
hollow coldness that invaded her stomach and the dizzy,
tingling flood of shock that swept through her limbs. She
sat up and then sat very still. Something had hit the car roof
— a terrific thud that made the car rock. It was followed by
an odd jostling noise that produced an echoing squeak from
the springs. She looked straight ahead at the road. The
darkness seemed to swarm in gouts of crepuscular particles
over the windscreen; cuts of sky were revealed and masked
and revealed again by the motion of the high branches.

The thud was a falling branch. A falling branch. It was a falling branch that the wind had brought down, it had dropped on to the roof of the car, it would be bound to make a hell of a noise because the trees were tall, but it was odd that she couldn't see any leaves or sprays of twig hanging out over the roof and that it hadn't then slipped to the ground and in any case what was the strange scuffling sound that followed and two miles walking and two miles jogging would make another half hour or so but he'd be more tired coming back. Oh God! And the noise came again.

She whimpered and heard herself doing it and realized that she was crying. The noise was less violent the second time. A thump. The same sort of noise, but more precisely located. It seemed to come from a point closer to the front of the roof than the back. She listened until the silence sang in her ears. She re-heard the noise in memory to try to identify it, rehearsing the intensity of the bang, its force and dull resonance and then the reality overlaid her recollection as it came again and then again and then again.

This time she did what she knew she would have to do. It was a compulsion. She didn't want to do it, so she looked up at the pocked plastic underside of the roof for a moment before raising her fist and placing the knuckles against the puffy lining. Then she drew her arm back and hammered a hysterical tattoo, through the padding, against the metal. There was a silence of about three or four seconds. Then a frenzied battering answered her.

Slowly, with the kind of care she might have taken in lifting a sleeping child, she raised her knees so that her heels were tucked under her on the seat, and wrapped her arms round her shins; then she lowered her head and thrust it between her raised knees and began to rock back and forth. Her crying was silent except for a tiny 'Aaah, aaah', uttered involuntarily with each little gathering of tears.

A car came towards her. She saw its lights from way off, a

47

halo of white on the crown of the road. She seemed to be
thinking carefully, logically, but it had travelled to within
fifty yards or so of her and she still hadn't moved. As it
approached, it slowed: the engine noise dropping to a low
burr. It had to be Peter, she reasoned. He had cadged a lift
from someone stopping at the garage. She waited for the
car to draw up on the opposite side of the road. It slowed
ever more − almost faltered; the lights were on full beam,
illuminating the interior of Peter's car, and it was no more
than a few feet away.

She came out of her foetal crouch and began to reach for
the door lock. Before she could touch it, the other car
crashed its gears and took off with such speed that the
bonnet seemed almost to lift in the air. As it passed her,
she caught a glimpse of two people, shadows, inside. Then
there was nothing but darkness, darker still after the
sudden illumination of headlights, and the faint sound of
the wind stirring the tall, stooping trees, and the empty
road. The sound came again: once, twice, three times and
then stopped.

The fear was so great now that she had almost lost her
ability to think rationally. She wanted to go to the lavatory
and wondered vaguely whether there would be one at the
garage if she started the car and drove on to join Peter there.
Her hand almost went out for the car key. Why hadn't he
been in the other car, the one that almost stopped? He
should have been in that car. She fiddled with an unravel-
ling thread on her sweater and then, on an impulse, pushed
her hand under the wool and clasped her own breast for
comfort's sake. They wouldn't have time to make love,
now. She wanted some distraction so she thought about
love-making, but there was nothing but coldness in her
because she was so afraid and the *thump, thump, thump,* on
the car roof came to make her feel sick and shake with
fright.

A single, sharp line of light curled around the interior of

the car like something alive and she shrieked. Then she saw
its source: it was a light on the road, approaching her,
coming quickly. Soon she could see that there were three,
perhaps four cars; two of them had lights on the roof that
revolved and flashed, spraying a glow to either side. That
was what she had noticed first, snaking past her face and
flicking on to the back window.

The police cars drew up all around her: one facing, two on
the opposite side of the road, one behind. The spinning
beacons fed an unearthly blue glow into the wood's interior, splashing on brush and bramble first on one side of the
road, then the other. The headlights were trained directly
on Peter's car, like floodlights on an historic building.
Jennie was unable to think. She waited.

The policemen were standing outside their cars. One of
them had an electric loud hailer. The sound of it seemed to
crack incoherently in her eardrums. She didn't react, so he
repeated his instruction: 'I want you to unlock the door, get
out of the car and walk towards me without looking back.
Get out. Walk quickly towards me. Look to the front.' She
listened while he said it a third time. Then she did it:
clambering over the gear stick to the driver's seat, pulling
up the lock, opening the door, stepping out, standing up,
walking half-way across the road into the blinding glare and
then – because she could do nothing to stop herself –
turning and looking back at the car.

The people in the car that had almost stopped – they
were the ones who had telephoned the police. They had
slowed on approaching Peter's car because what they had
seen had make them think, at first, that someone might
have had a break-down or an accident. Then they had
realized that that couldn't be – there was something wrong
about what seemed to be happening. There was something
bizarre, something manic about what they could see. Then
they had come a little closer and both guessed in the same
second. And as they drew almost level, they had seen. The

49

woman had said, 'Oh, dear God. Oh, Jesus,' as the man slammed the car into gear with a ferociously shaking hand and floored the accelerator. 'Oh, Christ. Oh, Jesus.' The woman's hand − in a reflexive gesture − had gone to her throat. Neither had spoken after that, until they had found the phone box.

It was very dark on the road, but they knew what they had seen and they knew why they had seen it. If Jennie had turned the radio on while waiting, or if Peter had been listening on his way to collect her, then she might have known too. It's lucky, perhaps, that she didn't; no one could have supported the knowledge, or spent almost twenty minutes with the suspicion. The radio would have told her that a madman had escaped from a nearby asylum after butchering two nurses with a cleaver stolen from the kitchen. The radio would have let her know that a gigantic search had been mounted in the area and that people were being advised to be very cautious indeed and told not, under any circumstances, to approach the man, who had been diagnosed homicidal and schizophrenic. The radio would also have given her the information that the man was dressed only in a white, institution gown. The couple in the car had seen the bare legs and the shapeless, ghostly-white smock before they had been able to make out clearly what was going on.

Jennie looked back. The man was crouching − kneeling but crouching over − on the roof of the car. They stared at each other for a moment; then she saw him smile, laughing silently, as he raised his arm and thumped down on the roof with what he held in his hand. The object made a thud. His fingers were twined into the hair to give him a grip; locked into the tangled hair of Peter's decapitated head. She felt the choke that comes before unconsciousness rising in her chest. Peter's face, blank, the eyes blankly open, mouth slack and twisted, all of it streaked with caked blood, a long flap of skin hanging from one side of the neck where the head had been hacked off − Peter's face looked at her. It would continue to look at her until the day she died.

Little Perry

The people of Upper Buccleigh had decided to tolerate the Glovers. As a rule, newcomers to the village were welcomed more or less unreservedly. They might never be fully accepted as locals, of course. It was necessary to live in the village for at least two decades before one could qualify even for honorary membership of that cabal with its short-hand of nods and grunts, its arcane reference to 'the flood back in '39', its encyclopaedic knowledge of scandals and lost fortunes, of open secrets and closed books. But few people moving into the place found themselves excluded from village activities or cold-shouldered in the pub: only those who were stand-offish themselves, or attempted to patronize with position or money.

The Glovers possessed no obvious failings of that sort. They were friendly, diffident, almost too anxious to please; but they were also — it had to be admitted — a distinctly *dotty* couple; almost weird. It had taken the villagers a little while to discover the fact, since the nature of the dottiness wasn't at first apparent.

It might have seemed rather strange that a couple of the Glovers' age should be the parents of a small child — Mrs Glover was clearly in her fifties, while her husband looked nearer his early sixties; strange, but not impossible. Odd, too, that though both parents spoke with unalloyed pride of 'little Perry', the boy was never with them when they went shopping on a Saturday morning or set off for a stroll after lunch on Sundays. One or two people who had visited the Glovers' house had looked in vain for any sign of the child, his toys, or books, or clothes. There were no tiny coats or boots in the hall, no engines, no plastic guns, or woollen animals, or scribbling blocks. Above all, there was no noise – no crying, nor yelling, no child's laughter from either up or downstairs.

In all this, the Glovers' little boy was something of a mystery; however, the village people felt they knew a great deal about the child: more than enough perhaps, since his parents were never so happy as when they were talking about him. Although he was only four years old and wouldn't start school for almost another year, Mrs Rogers, the headmistress of the village school, could never expect to meet the Glovers without having to renew her assurance that little Perry's place in the reception class was reserved for him. Similarly, shopkeepers and neighbours who were unwise enough to inquire about the boy were treated to a lengthy, shared monologue as Mr and Mrs Glover spoke with pride of how the baby had been a late blessing on their marriage, of their worries about his being an only child, of the care they had taken to choose a noble and traditional name ('Perry is just for now; he'll be Peregrine when he grows older'). It was necessary to hear of the mixture of excitement and concern they had felt when they had dis- covered that Mrs Glover ('Not exactly in the first flush, you know') had been carrying a child and of the way that apprehension had given way to joy. There was something embarrassing about the openness and insistence with which they described their emotions – the love they felt for their 'blessing'; it was, at the same time, both faintly aggressive and somehow sordid. Perhaps it was just this

53

excitement in the Glovers' voices when they talked about their son — something almost maniacal — that prevented people from being more openly curious. The unease the villagers felt when being harangued in street or shop made them want to get away from the couple and their obsession; and behind the edginess lay the inhibitions of social decorum: if a sense of eerie discomfort didn't prevent questions, then conventional politeness would. The questions were obvious, though; and if people neglected — or feared — to ask them of the Glovers, they certainly weren't averse to asking them of each other after the Glovers had gone.

May Botley was the first to realize what was going on. She and her husband, who managed the Hare and Hounds, were serving after-hours drinks to a select group of friends one evening and gossiping about village affairs. The talk got round to the Glovers and little Perry when May suddenly remarked, almost without seeming to expect contradiction, 'I don't think they've got a child at all.'

It stopped conversation dead. Eventually one of the other women found her voice. 'Good God, of course. I hadn't thought of that. Poor soul; oh dear, poor soul.' She meant, of course, Mrs Glover and the other women knew that. To be barren was to be less than a whole woman: a disappointment, a failure.

'But what about him?' asked May. 'Why should he go along with it? Shouldn't he do something about it — see that she gets some sort of . . . help? Tony, shouldn't he do that? Should we try to do something?'

Tony Edwards was the senior partner in Upper Buccleigh's medical practice. He waggled his glass, asking for a refill, then rubbed his jaw thoughtfully. 'I'm no psychotherapist . . . Sometimes it's better to simply leave these things alone. Inventing the child — if that's what they've done and now you mention it, all the evidence seems to point that way — is obviously a safety valve. It's harmless enough, really, isn't it? They depend on the fantasy to . . .

well . . . stay even, as it were. It doesn't hurt anyone. Actually, its not uncommon. Children invent playmates; people tell white lies about their past lives. Little Perry obviously fulfils a need in Mr and Mrs Glover. Making them face up to the truth might do untold damage for all I know. Let it lie.'

'But, look, what about *him*,' May persisted. 'Is he . . . I don't know . . . deluded too, or simply indulging her?'

'Who can say?' Tony shrugged. 'It probably started out as an indulgence and grew into something else. It's not un- usual for a couple who have been married — in the Glovers' case, what? — thirty years maybe, to have developed a kind of sixth sense, to be able to anticipate one another and possess a great sensitivity to each other's feelings. In just the same way, couples will share privacies . . . you know — little games, routines, pet names for things, a sort of code developed out of their history, their life together. My guess is that Mr Glover began by joining in his wife's game of "we've got a child" until it became more or less indistin- guishable from reality . . . *her* reality, in fact. It became second nature to fall in with her pretence; and after that became a comfort to him, too, I shouldn't wonder. If the self-deception has been going for some time — and it may have been, for all we know since they've lived in Buccleigh for only three months — then I should guess that it'd be almost as painful for him to admit that there *is* no child as it would be for his wife.'

May laughed. 'I thought you knew nothing about psychi- atry — wasn't that what you said?'

'Inspired amateurism, May. I'm a pro when it comes to distinguishing between malt whiskies, though. I wouldn't mind trying the Laphroaig this time. Any chance?'

The subject changed; but the deduction they had made about the imaginary infant soon spread through the village. Some thought it a distinctly unhealthy notion, but for the most part, people were inclined to be sympathetic even if the Glovers did, now that the truth was known, strike them as a little bizarre . . . even perhaps a little creepy. The couples' narrative of their son's progress, the obsessive way they worked him into every conversation, was met with smiles and nods, a 'Really?' or a 'How marvellous', which changed to pitying glances or good-natured gestures of irritation once the couple had moved on. They didn't become figures of fun, though, nor were they shunned, and if people didn't go out of their way to chat to them or make friends of them, they were none the less quick to remark (a shade patronizingly, perhaps) on the way that Mrs Glover managed to keep a house that was clearly too big for just the two of them meticulously clean and tidy, and on how well Mr Glover managed the garden. The Glovers would never be locals; but they would be tolerated.

And, indeed, accepted – almost entirely without rancour – as one of the odder aspects of life in Upper Buccleigh. As the summer wore on, there was the usual round of fêtes, garden parties, flower shows and church functions. Mrs Glover made fruit cakes for the Women's Institute stall; Mr Glover won third prize with his dahlias at the flower show; they helped at the bring-and-buy sales and went to church almost every Sunday. On warm evenings they could be seen, over the thick privet hedge that bordered their property, hoeing and weeding and pruning. No one minded too much any more the gleeful accounts of little Perry's progress; but no one, of course, laid eyes on little Perry, and the hidden, knowing smiles still followed the polite demonstrations of interest.

Only Tony Edwards, the doctor, had realized that a moment of truth would arrive: the day when little Perry was due to begin his education at the village school. The realization worried him. He half-expected the Glovers to leave the village before then, assuming that other, similar, moments must have arrived in other places and guessing that the couple's dependence on the myth of little Perry would force them to flee rather than admit the truth either to themselves or others. He had this sad vision of Mr and Mrs Glover settling more or less happily in place after place, boasting of their child, blinding themselves to the kindness, the disbelief, the pity or the contempt of those they lived among, then uprooting themselves and moving on before the lie was exposed and the kindness could turn to awkward embarrassment, the disbelief to scorn, the pity to irritation and the contempt to aggression.

Each day, as the beginning of the school term grew dangerously close, Tony waited to hear that the Glovers had found an excuse to leave the village. Little Perry's education, perhaps, or a decision to live abroad. They would go, he thought, as they had come: quietly, with no fuss, unobserved since their house lay at the far end of the village, well away from the centre. Then, a week or so before the term was due to start, he heard something that caused him real concern. The Glovers had been to the High Street on a shopping spree. They had bought a maroon-coloured blazer, grey shorts and a maroon-and-silver tie — the school uniform — together with a pencil box, ruler and other classroom necessities. Mrs Rogers had been visited and queried about what else might be needed. The experience had upset her a good deal.

That same evening, after surgery finished, Mrs Rogers paid Tony Edwards a visit. 'It's all very distressing,' she said, sipping at the sherry he had given her. 'Very unsettling. I really didn't know what to say.'

'What *did* you say?' Tony asked her.

'Well, what they wanted to hear, really. Do you suppose that it was the wrong thing to do? I didn't think it right to let them know that it's common knowledge — their imaginary child, I mean; it's not really my place; and in any case I was anxious not to . . . well . . . disturb them in any way. Do you follow?'

'Of course. I'm sure you were right. If they are to be

57

confronted with their own self-deception − that is, if it's going to be necessary to force them to come clean before things get to the point of no return − then it's going to have to be done with enormous care and tact.'

'And it is going to be necessary, isn't it?' chipped in Tony's wife, Beth, as she strolled over to replenish Mrs Rogers's glass. 'Sooner rather than later, someone is going to have to bring things out into the open.'

'Yes.' Tony held out his own glass. 'Yes, it is. If they continue to act as if little Perry were about to make his first public appearance at school in − what − '

'Just over a week,' responded Mrs Rogers.

' − then it's likely that they themselves will grow more and more desperate as the day comes closer. They've trapped themselves by extending the fantasy this far; I feel desperately sorry for them; what can they do, though, if they want to stay in the village, but proceed in the direction that their lie must take them? It's unstoppable, now. I wouldn't be surprised to discover that they're both in a state of panic underneath it all. Anyway, within a week or so, they'll be exposed to everyone − including themselves, if you see what I mean.'

'They could delay that; invent stories for little Perry's absence on the first day of school − illness, or whatever.'

'They could, Beth,' agreed Tony, 'but they sure as hell couldn't keep it up for ever. And the longer they delayed, the more lies they told, then the more ridiculous they'd finally seem; and the more desperate they'd become. No; better if the whole thing is faced before it goes any further. It's obvious that they're going to go on with this business of buying uniforms and whatnot. Someone will have to do something.'

'Who?'

'Yes − ' Mrs Rogers added her query to Beth's, 'who's going to be the one to . . . ' Her voice trailed away.

'It won't be me,' Tony said firmly, getting up to pour

another drink. 'I can speculate about the reasons for the Glovers' behaviour well enough and I can guess at what might be the result of this or that course of action. Fine. But I'm no expert in this sort of thing; and in any case − sheer cowardice − I really don't want it on my plate.'

'It's logical that you should do it,' Mrs Rogers said. 'Family physician and all that; and you *do* seem to have some theories about the Glovers.'

'Not me.' Tony shook his head. 'Really; not me. If anything, it's a spiritual matter more than anything else. I'm strictly a splints and penicillin man. I think the vicar should do it.'

'Yes, that seems reasonable,' agreed Beth. 'He'd be good in the "care and tact" department. He knows all about the business, I imagine?' Tony and Beth weren't churchgoers. They knew the vicar well enough from various village functions, from greetings and short chats in the street, but could scarcely be called friends of the Reverend Davidson.

'Oh yes, he knows,' Mrs Rogers assured them. 'He's as concerned as anyone − ' she paused; − ' more, I should imagine. They both go to church pretty regularly, you know.'

'The vicar should do it,' said Tony firmly.

John Davidson didn't want to perform the task any more than Tony did. He knew he would have to, though. Something of a conference had been held at the pub, after which the Reverend Davidson had been visited by Tony Edwards and Mrs Rogers, who had given him the latest developments and described the problem. It was a test − he knew it was a test. Since he had arrived in the parish some five years before, life had gone on smoothly and more or less without incident. Not that he had expected Divine Revelation any more than he had imagined that his faith would be challenged by hardship or deprivation or any overt manifestation of the Devil and all his works. John Davidson

59

wasn't a proselytizer or a failed mystic; he enjoyed the calm and uneventfulness of the quiet parish and possessed little or no desire to suffer the turbulence, the doubt or the ecstasy of those who wrestled with their own souls. John's was a simple, secure faith that flourished best in the mild soil and temperate climate of an English village. He was more than content to leave to others the deserts of denial and the winnowing flame of self-doubt. A tolerant and meek man, he preached, to his tiny congregations each Sunday, the love of a tolerant and meek Saviour.

So the problem of little Perry — and the need to resolve that problem — left him with a chill weight in the pit of his stomach. To give him praise where due, he had sat with the dying and prayed with the bereaved as part of his normal parish duties, and had never avoided them, much as they disturbed him. He realized, too, that the task ahead of him scarcely called for the courage and selfless submission to anguish of the martyrs; but none the less he shrank from it. It took much of his nerve and determination to get him to the Glovers' front door and ring the bell.

'I've come to talk to you about . . . it's about your son,' he said after the pleasantries had been exchanged. Mrs Glover returned from the kitchen where she had been making a pot of tea. 'About your son,' he said again, as he accepted the cup. Mr Glover offered biscuits fussily arranged on a decorated china plate. '. . . About his going to school next week.'

Mr Glover sat down on the sofa, facing the vicar. 'Yes, he'll be starting next week; that's right.'

His wife sat alongside him, balancing her cup. 'We've got everything he needs,' she added. 'Uniforms and what have you. I think he's looking forward to it, don't you, Alfred?'

Davidson watched Glover for any sign of hesitancy or nervousness; there was none. 'I believe he is, yes.' Husband and wife smiled at the vicar and waited to hear what he had come to say.

'It's just that . . .' John Davidson hadn't any plan of what

he would say or how he would say it. There had seemed no
way to prepare for an encounter such as this. Now that the
moment had arrived, he couldn't bring himself to be blunt.
He said — in as soft and kind a tone as he could muster —
'Mrs Glover, I wonder if I could meet little Perry.' Even as
the words left him, he felt afraid; and when he had spoken,
he waited with a mixture of pity and guilt and acute embarrassment for whatever effect his request would have on the
couple.

Mrs Glover smiled again. 'Of course you can, Vicar.'
She put down her teacup and got up; her husband followed
suit. 'Of course. That would be lovely. Come along.'

Davidson followed Mr and Mrs Glover up the stairs to a
landing that gave on to the three principal bedrooms. At the
far end, past the furthest bedroom, was a door with a
hook-and-eye catch. This Glover unlocked and the three of
them climbed the narrow stairway that led to the attic.
Davidson simply didn't know what to think; he followed as
he was bidden; in so far as it's ever possible, his mind was a
blank. Another hook-and-eye catch was fixed to the attic
door. Mrs Glover unhooked it and swung the door back.
'Perry,' she said softly. 'Perry, my love, here's someone to
see you.'

It was a child. It was a child that scraped and flopped
across the bare boards of the attic towards him. Davidson
could see that it was a child. Even as he recoiled from the
rank smell of urine that scorched his nostrils, from the
terrible drag and dull slap of the child's progress — a sound
that would fill his dreams and bring him awake, yelling;
even as he smelled and heard these things, he could see
that, yes, it was a child.

The child must have been born almost entirely without
bones, apart from its backbone. The flesh puddled and
hung in obscene, livid white sacs, falling pendulously from
the warped column of its spine. Obviously there was some
strength in its arms, because it used them to haul itself

61

across the floor to where Davidson stood, trembling and sick and bathed in a cold sweat. Its face was an obscene flap of wrinkled skin, matted with thick, dark down and pocked with random holes that were eyes, nose, mouth. Slowly, inexorably, it flapped and wallowed towards him until it came to rest with a gruesome rolling of blubber some two or three feet away.

'Here's little Perry, Vicar,' said Mrs Glover, her voice light and pleased, full of maternal pride.

'Perry for now,' Mr Glover put in, chuckling warmly. 'Peregrine when he grows older.' Both parents gazed down fondly at the child, their smiles broad, their eyes alight with a love devoid of sorrow or sanity or fear.

The Reverend Davidson gripped the door-post as faintness and nausea swept over him. For a brief moment of appalled lucidity, it occurred to him to wonder what it was the Glovers could see, there, on the floor: what image of the child they held in minds dislocated by horror and duped by love. He fought to keep his voice even, to keep it from curdling in the bile that rose in his throat.

'Well,' he said. 'Hullo, Perry. Hullo.' His hand tightened on the door frame until he thought the bones would break.

A Testing Time

June Sheldon was a passionate girl. She was twenty-one, had a striking figure and a pertly pretty face framed by naturally wavy hair that she wore long, sometimes fastening it back into a pony-tail so that her high cheek-bones were accentuated. She was unattached, though there was no shortage of young men in her life, many of them good-looking or charming or rich, or all three. She had little time for any of them: her passion got in the way. June was passionate about motor bikes.

When she was fifteen, her elder brother had let her ride pillion for a mile or so on the 500cc Triumph he had recently bought. It seemed then – it still seemed – the most exciting thing she could imagine. Since that time, her life had been bikes: reading about them, stripping them down and re-assembling them, repairing them, going regularly to rallies and cross-country events, to scrambles and speedway, treating herself to an annual trip, along with other enthusiasts, to the Isle of Man.

She had never owned a bike – although she could ride – nor had she bothered to pass her driving test, because she was saving herself for the moment when a dream could come true: when she could afford the bike that featured in the dream, the bike she drooled over in showrooms, the bike whose modifications she followed from year to year in the magazines. June wanted a 250cc Ducati.

If someone wants something badly enough, the world will sometimes conspire to keep it from him, until desire has become frenzy, and frenzy, finally, becomes something sour and murky, a bitter parody of that first, fierce attraction. Desire, then, becomes a desire to destroy. To the rich and powerful, of course, the world will often grant what is wanted at once — with ease — and soon those people will want nothing, will care for nothing; eagerness will turn to boredom, fascination to disdain. But every now and then, the world will grant to someone that he gets what he desires before the yearning can turn to spite, but not soon enough to blunt the fine edge of lust. The world isn't often that perfect, but it favoured June that way. Her twenty-first birthday present, contributed to by her family, her relations, and everyone she knew, was a Ducati 250.

The first thing she had done on that birthday morning was to ride the bike to her local county offices and put in for her test. After that, she went to her bank and drew out almost all her savings. This was not a bike she would ride in the gear she had been making do with for the past few years; *this* bike deserved something special. The leathers that she bought were black with dark-red markings: a double stripe along the side seams of the jacket and trousers, with a flash descending from either shoulder of the jacket and ending at the waistband. Her new helmet was black with a full visor and matching flashes on both sides. They would be worn, she had decided, on the day of her test. She knew that she would pass with no trouble; but the gear would stay in her wardrobe until she could think of herself as a fully-fledged rider.

Now the day had arrived when she would put the leathers on for the first time. At breakfast, her family was tactful, careful not to be unnaturally quiet, but careful, too, that there should be no mention of the test. No one would make the mistake of wishing her good luck, or expressing the hope that all would go well — no jinxes of that sort. June smiled to herself. She knew what was going on, but it didn't throw her. She was confident, utterly unworried; maybe just a touch impatient, though; eager to take off the L-plates that spoiled the look of the bike and throw them into the dustbin.

She reached the test-centre a few minutes early. Her examiner was a mild, middle-aged man with sandy hair and a kind smile. He seemed impressed by the bike — and impressed, too, by June's handling of it. She was sailing through the test and she knew it.

'Now,' he said smilingly, as she drew up at the kerb after some minutes of manoeuvring, 'I want you to ride down the road here and take the first left turn, then the next, then the next, so that you've ridden three sides of a square. I'll be waiting in this street to our right. As you approach, I shall step out in front of you; I want you to stop as quickly as you can. The emergency stop. O.K.?'

June nodded and set off. It took her just a few minutes to make the partial circuit and enter the third street. Ahead of her, she saw a small group of people bunched by the side of the road and in the middle of them, a motor cyclist. He was wearing black leathers with red piping, a black helmet, with dark-red flashes, one on either side. The examiner lay a few feet from his front wheel, unmoving, a thick seepage of blood issuing from his ear. June drew up alongside the other rider and lifted her visor. The man looked at her with eyes dulled by shock; he made no attempt to get off his bike, or to turn off the engine. The crackle and throb of the two Ducati 250s were the only sounds, until someone bending over the examiner said: 'I think he's dead. Has anyone sent for an ambulance?'

'He must have been crazy,' the man removed his helmet with trembling hands. 'I hadn't a chance to stop. He step-

65

ped out − ' Then the shock in his eyes was succeeded by something like horror as he took in June's leathers, the red flashes, the helmet with its decorations and dark, plexiglass visor, the bike she was sitting on. He spoke the rest of the sentence slowly, scarcely aware that the words were leaving his slack lips. ' − right . . . right in front . . . of . . . me.' June switched her engine off. She started to cry. They could all hear, in the distance but getting nearer, the whoop and wail of a siren, strengthening, then rising to screaming-pitch.

Quick Change

'Over here, Gerry!' Frank Watson was waving from the far end of the open-plan office, one hand held high to indicate his position, the other stroking the hip of Sally Freeman, the 'permanent temp'. Gerry Lawson screwed the top back on to the gin bottle and lobbed it to Chris Murray; Chris dummied it behind his back, then flicked it to Dot Hamilton; Dot threw it two-handed to Frank. Frank splashed two trebles into paper cups, for himself and Sally, then waved at Gerry once more and winked extravagantly.

It was just after noon, it was Christmas Eve, the publicity office was festooned with paper-chains and streamers and obscene balloons and strings of Christmas cards, the party had been under way for a half-hour or so and the joint — as Fats Waller might have observed — was really jumping. It was also being passed from hand to hand at the far end of the office and Gerry thought that he might well trot down there, in a minute or two, and sample 'certain substances' for the first time. He felt elated and mildly depressed simultaneously. At first he couldn't determine why this should be; then he realized that he was drunk, but not drunk enough. He had reached the maudlin stage, but depression was held at bay by the sheer weight of jollity about the place.

They staged a Christmas party every year: collections were made to pay for the booze, the secretaries spent half a morning arranging the decorations and the Head of Department — after downing the token drink and wishing everyone a Merry Christmas — did the decent thing and went home before midday so that the revelry would be uninhibited by the presence of a 'boss'. The cleaners always complained, even though a tenner was left out for them amid the debris. And everything else that was traditionally supposed to happen at an office party happened. A few people became ill, a few home truths were told, Frank Watson (who would have benefited from a crash-course in keeping his mouth shut) pledged to tell the management what buffoons they were, secretaries were groped — usually uncomplainingly — and two or three ill-advised adulteries took place between people who woke up the next morning hating themselves and each other and wondering how on earth they would be able to salvage pride, equanimity and status.

Gerry watched Frank's hand snaking and climbing while Sally, apparently unperturbed, talked and laughed with somebody on her other side; then he took a hefty pull on his gin. That swallow — and the next — made all the difference. He felt the depression drift away and a small but definable recklessness take over. He would go home: yes. He would catch the five-twenty-seven: yes. He would accompany Laura to a boring dinner at the boring house of Karen and Andrew Brownlow, the local bores. Yes. But he'd make his mark, too. If he maintained this level of gentle drunkenness, he could be spitefully witty, cool, withdrawn and devastatingly critical by turns, demonstrating his displeasure at being there without becoming embarrassing, his contempt for them all without being openly hostile. He was rather looking forward to it. Boring bloody people. Boring bloody Laura.

Ten years, give a couple of months: and the last five

anniversaries had been memorable for their rancour. Gerry recollected the last one and winced. 'Marriage red in tooth and claw' was how he had described it a day or so later, over a small lake of whisky, while his best friend, Fred Naylor, sat patiently listening to his dreary monologue.

'It's not me, for Christ's sake,' he had muttered across the rim of his over-full glass. 'Laura just can't stop. Can't stop. She's a world-class nag, boy; I should have guessed when I first met her sodding mother. Together, they could rule the world, d'you know that? Laura's poor father . . . if the old woman says "Jump" he doesn't wait to ask how high. Hen-pecked? Christ! He's got a permanent carapace of scar-tissue. And she's just the same. Laura. Just the bloody same. If I won the Nobel Peace Prize I'd get hell for having to go to Sweden to collect it. If I dig the garden, I should have cleaned the windows too. If I'm home late − if I've stayed on at the office − I'm neglecting her; if I'm home early I'm squandering my chances of promotion; if I go to bed early, I'm insensitive to the fact that she's spent all day in the house alone and wants somebody to talk to; if I stay up late, I'm rejecting her. Don't smoke in the bedroom, don't drive so fast, don't express an opinion, don't be stand-offish . . . if I slashed my wrists in the bath she'd be there, just catching me before I floated into blissful bloody oblivion, yelling at me for being inconsiderate enough to leave a tide-mark round the rim.'

He had watched while Fred patiently re-filled his glass and made sympathetic noises. 'I don't know what to do. I've had enough, though, I can tell you that.'

Almost a year had passed and nothing had changed. In truth, it had to be admitted − Fred admitted it, other friends admitted it − Laura was equipped with a sharp tongue, a short fuse and a talent for selfishness that attained gold-medal standards. They had stopped calling round at Gerry's house: stopped thinking of Gerry and Laura as a couple. Privately, they had speculated on how much longer the marriage would last; and even more privately, they had admitted that their sympathy for Gerry was mixed with a certain amount of disdain for the way he put up with the seven-day-a-week, fifty-two-weeks-a-year bitching. In fact, Gerry endured it all because deep down, below the level of simple resentment and mere pique, Laura scared him stiff.

He had promised himself a drag on that bulky, home-rolled cigarette with the intriguing flavour, so he weaved between the couples bopping to five-year-old Beatles records, lifted the smouldering joint from between the slender fingers of a pretty blonde from the typing-pool and sucked smoke down through clenched teeth, holding it in his lungs as he had seen others do. He felt nothing – passed the joint back and leaned over to kiss the girl as she accepted it. She laughed through the kiss, but her mouth opened. He felt her tongue dance along his teeth, dabbing, then riding up under his lip.

Without knowing quite how it happened, he found himself dancing with her, swivelling and rolling his shoulders among the milling couples in twenty square feet of floor-space where the desks had been cleared away. He watched her small breasts bob with that strange, erotic treble motion that only small breasts achieve: rise-drop-swell; rise-drop-swell. She was wearing a turquoise dress slit to mid-thigh on either side, and she concentrated on her dancing, smiling at him only now and then. He tried to remember her name and whether there was an office in the building with a lock on the door. Then she was gone, and the music was different and he was sitting on the edge of a desk with a drink in his hand while Frank Watson swayed to and fro before him, entering and leaving his field of clear vision as his voice tuned in and out.

'First bloody thing on our first morning back in the office, I'll be in to see him . . . appointment and he agreed. I told them all a dozen . . . last sales conference . . . listen? No! If

they'd . . . I told them then, things would have been . . .
time I won't pull my punches . . . department's run on
entirely the wrong . . . idiot — damn near lost us the . . .
happened if they'd listened to . . . '

Gerry smiled and nodded, organizing his cup under the
shaky stream of gin from Frank's bottle. His leg felt numb,
so he slid off the desk intending to stand up and flex the
limb. He found himself on the floor, sitting upright with his
back against the leg of the desk. A gout of gin from the
still-levelled bottle cascaded down his lapel and soaked the
top of his trousers. The blonde sat down beside him and
lodged a new joint in his mouth. He dragged, inhaled and
offered it back by puckering his lips, then made a clumsy
lunge at her, dropping his cup into his lap. The lunge was
overdone and they knocked heads. She didn't retreat at
once. She took the now empty paper cup out of his lap,
kissed him, ran her tongue over his face in a swift, surprising gesture, then took his hand and placed it against her
breast, rotating it briskly as if she were greasing a baking
tin. Then she hopped to her feet, poured more gin into his
cup, handed it to him and pushed off through the dancers.

He drank the gin and went to look for her, taking great
care to walk steadily — one foot in line with the other,
correcting his lurches before they carried him off balance —
and trying to keep the gyroscope of a room in true. When he
found her, she was lip to lip, clavicle to clavicle and groin to
groin with Philip Jones, the department's space-buyer. His
hand was through the slit in her dress, hiking it up slightly
as he cupped her buttock; her knee was between his legs,
rising and falling like someone pumping a tyre. Gerry
turned round too quickly and sat down. When he got up,
someone filled his cup for him. It was Scotch, but he drank
it down blindly. He felt damn good.

The Beatles had given way to the Rolling Stones, streamers were floating and spiralling through the air, mistletoe
was being waved above the heads of all and sundry and

71

someone had broken the back of a chair. He danced with half-a-dozen girls, keeping his balance more often than not, and when not, allowing his partner to help him to his feet so that he could stroke her from knee to neck before resuming the dance. He drank from whichever cup was nearest. Then, all at once, he didn't feel quite so good after all. In fact, he felt like hell and he had to get out of the room and if he hurried he'd just make it. And Oh, Christ!

The landing outside was cold and silent and had a floor made of marshmallow. He made it to the lift, got inside, sat down after pressing the button for the seventh floor where the lavatories were, and then went to sleep immediately. When he woke up, ten minutes later, he was looking at a large number seven painted on the wall opposite the lift doors. He was sick three times without moving. The lift doors closed and he started to descend. When the doors opened again, the wall bore a large '3': his floor. Frank Watson peered at him through a fog of liquor. 'Oh dear, Oh Lor'.' He laughed girlishly. 'Oh dear dear dear.' The doors closed and the lift mechanism whined. Before they got back to seven, Gerry had been sick twice.

Half-propping, half-pushing, Frank Watson steered Gerry into the men's room. They were in there for a very long time. When they emerged, Gerry felt pale and weak, shaky and ill, and sober. And wretched. He put Frank back into the lift and sought out an empty office, where he sat down to formulate a plan of action. It was five-fifteen and he had as good as missed his train; in addition to that, his suit and shirt were disgusting beyond belief. He was terrified. They would be late for the Brownlows' dinner, he stank, his clothes were foul, Laura would give him hell, he hated himself and he was terrified.

After five minutes of desperate thinking, he began to see a way of saving the day. He needed two things: an excuse for being late and some new clothes . . . and a reason for wearing new clothes. Factor three. He brightened. The office party, where things had got out of hand: people acting stupidly. A pot of ink spilled right across his suit. Vast apologies and offers to pay for dry-cleaning on the part of the miscreant. A trip to a nearby clothes store − funded by the ink-spiller − to buy cheap cords, a shirt and a jacket. Which sortie had made him miss the train. No! He had been in time for the train, but it had been cancelled because the driver hadn't turned up for work − even better. One irritation after another. That way, he could act injured, put-upon, weary and annoyed. He would have to move fast in order to catch the six-seventeen, but it was just on. He strode to the lift, descended to the third floor, snatched his nylon anorak from the rack outside the office, then set off at a fast clip for the clothes shop three streets away.

Pushing through the double glass doors, he walked swiftly across the ladies' department, past the cashier and ascended the steps to the men's department three at a time. It took him no more than five minutes to select a pair of medium-sized corduroy trousers, a plain shirt − 16″ collar − and a cheap linen jacket that he shrugged into and out of in a matter of seconds behind the batwing slats of the changing-room door. The assistant popped them into a brightly-coloured cardboard carrier with a string loop to close it and scribbled out a bill. Gerry waited, hopping with impatience. He was conscious of the fact that the assistant must have been able to detect the pungent, unmistakable odour wafting from beneath the anorak, but his embarrassment was nothing beside his eagerness to get on to the street, into a taxi and *en route* for the station. He would have liked to have changed into the new clothes there and then, but he knew that would mean a trip to the cashier, then another back to the changing room, where he would lose precious minutes unpacking and unpinning the shirt. Time was too short for that − and taxis were scarce. He would have to phone Laura from the station, too, so that his story held up.

73

At the cashier's desk, he waited in line behind three women who were fussing, one after the other, with store credit cards. Their carrier-bags lay on the counter-top while the cashier phoned the accounts department to check the credit limit of each woman. Gerry shifted from foot to foot and looked at his watch.

'Could I . . . ?' He put his bag down and went to the front of the queue and fished out his wallet, extracting three ten- and three five-pound notes. 'I'm in a terrible hurry.' The women regarded him stonily: the stained trouser legs, the flaxen face. 'Sorry. I'm going to miss a train. Could I . . . Sorry.' He plonked down the money and the bill, reached over and grabbed his bag, then made to leave.

'Sixteen, eight and twenty,' said the cashier. 'You've got some change.'

'That's O.K.' He was at the door, pushing it open. 'It's O.K. Merry Christmas to you.' Clutching the carrier under his arm, he ran to a nearby set of traffic lights at a crossroads and looked left and right for a taxi. It was almost dark and a light drizzle was falling.

For five minutes, he stood on the corner without seeing a taxi going in any direction, for hire or not, and he was beginning to panic. Then God permitted a miracle and three, each with its yellow light glowing in the false city dusk, approached the crossroads. He flagged down the leader, got in, and said, 'I need to be at Victoria in ten minutes.' As the cabbie turned to protest, Gerry thrust his last fiver through the partition.

It took twelve minutes, which gave him five to get the train. The second miracle was a telephone that functioned. He dialled, dancing with frustration as the ringing tone drilled on and on, then heard Laura's voice.

'Train cancelled,' he gabbled, 'getting the next one. Still be in reasonable time if we hurry. Explain later.'

Waving his season-ticket, he raced through the barrier and slammed into the nearest carriage. As the door closed, so the train began to move. Gasping, he sank into a seat. His legs felt very uncertain indeed and his heart seemed to be missing one beat in three − but he had made it! He watched the bleak rows of dingy house-backs drift past and wondered vaguely whether the office party was still lurching anarchically on. The passenger next to him stirred and shifted away and Gerry was reminded of the state of his clothes; in the overheated carriage a thin, rank smell was beginning to flow from him and people were staring at the dry, crumbly stains on his trouser legs.

He got up and went out into the corridor, walking like a man on shipboard along the length of the train, looking for a vacant lavatory. The first two were occupied, and the next set of two. He waited outside for what seemed an age, then gave up and went further along the train. After another five minutes of fruitless searching, he came to an empty compartment right at the head of the train. Sliding the door open, he went in, flopping into a window seat and wedging his elbow on to the narrow sill so that he could support his head. Suddenly he felt unwell − the need to buy new clothes and catch the train had provided enough adrenalin to keep him going, but now exhaustion and a lingering biliousness took over. His head was thumping dully; muscles were jumping and flickering in his calves; a feeling of ill-being sluiced through him like a grey, flotsam-choked tide. He closed his eyes against the onslaught of neon.

He woke with a terrific jump, as if his brain − in order to warn him − had spasmed his entire frame, bringing him half out of his seat. He cupped his hands round his face, leaned against the window and read the countryside for a geographical fix. Commuters, it seems, develop a strange kind of sixth sense. They can enjoy a deep sleep from the moment they board the train until three minutes before it draws into their home stations, or tell from the black smudge of countryside funnelling past the window exactly where they are. Gerry knew that he had only a couple of minutes before the train would stop and he would have to get off; he also knew it was a fair bet that Laura would be waiting on the platform — the car nearby — impatient to get him home and then swiftly on to the Brownlows'. Even as he thought it, the train appeared to lose speed slightly, slowing down for the approach.

The carriage was still empty: unsurprisingly, since only a handful of regulars travelled that far down the line. He leaped to his feet, tore off the anorak and dropped it on to the floor, then stripped off jacket, trousers, tie and shirt. Grimacing with revulsion, he wadded the reeking mess of clothing into a ball, yanked open one of the sliding ventilation windows and rammed it through. The clothes separated as they fell, flicking back in the slipstream. The white sail of his shirt billowed and tumbled along the gravel.

Gerry tore the lip of the carrier-bag out of its string fastening and tipped the contents on to the seat. His eyes widened with horror and he put a hand up to the overhead rack for support, but he didn't speak. He simply stood there in his socks and shoes and Y-fronts, wondering, with the kind of sinister, calm curiosity that precedes hysteria, which of the women in the store had gone home with a pair of corduroys, a shirt and a linen jacket. On the seat before him lay a pale blue winceyette dressing-gown decorated with small sprays of flowers, a black nylon half-slip edged with lace, a peach-coloured bra and a peach-coloured suspender-belt to match.

The Windfall

Paddy would know what to do: Paddy, it often seemed, had the answer to just about everything. There was little that Paddy couldn't pronounce on; few problems he couldn't solve and very few difficulties he couldn't overcome. 'I'll ask Paddy,' Bill Wallace told his wife. 'Paddy'll come up with something.'

'Let's hope so,' she said. 'We can't get on with making something of the cellar until those bloody things have been moved. I want some space down there for myself, you know, as well as you and the boys.'

'I know that. Don't worry.' Bill sliced the top off his boiled egg and inspected the surface for 'gup'; he couldn't eat 'guppy' eggs, the soft, nacreous slime turned his stomach. 'Paddy will sort it out.'

'What sort of barrels?' Paddy asked him later that day, as they sat over lunch at the office local. 'How big?'

'Bloody enormous. I should think about eight feet from top to bottom, and four feet or more across.'

'How the hell did they get there?'

'You tell me.' He lifted Paddy's glass and raised an eyebrow; Paddy nodded and he went to the bar for another round. When he came back, Paddy was deep in thought.

'Cut them up,' he said. 'Or saw them in two and give the halves to Mary for plants and the like. Look very pretty outside the front door.'

'You haven't been listening, have you?' Bill accused. 'That's exactly what we want to do. But the damn things weigh a ton a piece; *ergo*: there is something in them and we don't know what.'

'Liquid?' asked Paddy hopefully.

'Difficult to tell. Could it be?'

'Could be anything, I suppose. Liquid often does come in barrels — interesting liquid at that. How long do you suppose they've been there?'

Bill gave the question some thought. 'Well, they were there when we moved in last month. No one mentioned them, not the estate agents, nor the surveyor. The last people obviously weren't troubled by them, but I don't think they actually put them there; if they had, then they would presumably have made use of whatever is inside. In any case, it was clear from the state of the place that no one had put the cellar to any practical purpose for generations.'

'But you want to?'

'Yes, and so do Mary and the boys. We've each got our plans for the space. Mary will have her potter's wheel down there, the boys can use a bit of it as a workroom, and I — '

'You can put the billiard table you're lusting after down there.'

'Exactly.' Bill smiled wryly. 'I've waited long enough for that table. The whole point of moving to the country, and going through the misery of commuting, was so that we could all have more space: a bigger house, more room for everyone.'

'And now you find you've inherited eight dirty-great barrels full of the unknown and they're cramping your style.' Paddy grinned at him.

'Mmmm, indeed.' Bill looked thoughtful. 'I wonder how long they have been there. I mean, the house is Victorian, but it's built on the site of a much older place, you know. They could have been there for donkey's years for all I know.' He cupped his chin in his hand. 'I wonder what *is* in them.'

'Have they got bungs?' demanded Paddy.

'I don't know.' Bill considered a moment. 'Probably. Yes, I think so. Don't all barrels have them?'

'We'll tap them,' Paddy decided.

'Tap them?'

'We'll borrow the wherewithal from that chummy bod that runs your local, and we'll tap them. Who knows, boy, they might be full of brandy.'

They weren't. They were full of rum. That weekend, Paddy stayed with the Wallaces. The landlord of the Bunch of Grapes gave them a quick lesson in how to use the tackle he had lent them, after which they went back to the house, straight down to the cellar, tapped the nearest barrel and drew off a pint or so of fluid into the saucepan that Bill had brought along for the purpose. They didn't need to taste it to know what it was. The sweet, unmistakable bouquet of dark rum filled the cellar. But they tasted it none the less.

'Jesus, it's rum,' Paddy laughed. 'You've got gallons and gallons of rum here, boy. You lucky beggar.'

There were mixed feelings about the amount of luck involved. 'It's all very nice,' said Mary, 'but they're still taking my potting space. Anyway, I don't much like rum. Do you?'

'In point of fact,' Bill observed, 'yes, I do. Look, let's leave them there for the next month or so − until the billiard table arrives. We'll drink as much of the stuff as we can − or as much as we want to − then I'll get Paddy to help me to siphon the stuff off over a weekend and we'll flog it to Andy at the Grapes. How does that sound? I'm going to be too busy for the next few weeks to do anything about it. At least we know they'll be going fairly soon; and, in the meantime,

79

we can get sozzled on free rum every night. In fact,' the realization had only just come to him, 'we're bound to make quite a profit from it all. Do look on the bright side.'

Mary nodded. 'Sounds reasonable. O.K.' She grinned. 'More than O.K., when I come to think about it. Well, well; quite a little windfall, really, isn't it?'

For the next month, they drank a great deal of rum. In addition to which, they had more than their fair share of rum truffles, rum butter, rum-based sauces and other ingeniously adapted delicacies. They even made a few rum ice-lollies.

'Frankly,' Bill told Paddy one day as he arrived at the office, 'I'm getting a little fed up with rum.'

'I can imagine,' said Paddy. 'Well, to be honest, I can't; but I see what you mean. It's this weekend, isn't it?'

'If you can make it.'

'Sure. I'll enjoy it. Can I sip as I go?'

Bill laughed. 'Of course. Just don't get too blotto to help me finish the job. The billiard table goes in on Monday, or it stands outside suffering the weather.'

It didn't take them too long to drain the first barrel. While Bill lugged the plastic jerrycans of rum to one corner of the cellar, Paddy revved the small chain-saw he had brought with him. Bill came over to help, rolling the tun sideways when Paddy had made a cut that half-divided it. They cut the rest and Bill yanked at his side.

The body was almost black. Its upper torso protruded from the barrel, the head a wrinkled, prune-like nub, the arms stiff at its sides, the legs, still in a slop of rum, mummi-fied and rigid. The leathery skin stretched tightly over the rib-cage, then sank to a thick pouch of stomach. The two men looked at it wordlessly. Then Bill walked over to the wall and was sick for a long time.

Paddy discovered the answer − of course. In the pub, at lunchtime on the following Monday, he explained it to Bill. 'Not uncommon practice, it appears. People who died in the Colonies, boy — they often got that treatment. See, if the body was being sent back to England for burial, rum was the best preservative, and the cheapest. Jamaica, that one might have come from. Funny how it got overlooked, though. Must have puzzled the bereaved, don't you think?' He laughed loudly. 'Oh dear, oh dear. I'll always remember the look on Mary's face when we told her. All that rum butter! Oh dear.' When he had finished laughing, he picked up Bill's glass. 'Have a refill?' he asked.

'I think I will,' Bill said. 'Make it a brandy.'

The Outing

'Woods, seaside, funfair, waxworks,' said Sidney Andrews as he propped his youngest son on his blue plastic potty, 'or the cinema.'

'Or the safari park,' countered his wife. 'They'd like the safari park.'

'Yes? Oh well — or the safari park.' Baby Nicholas sat and stared at his father and went pink in the face. His brother Darren, who was eight, came into the room. 'We want the safari park,' he announced. By 'we' he meant himself and his elder brother, Geoff.

'Do you? I see.' Sid watched the baby's colour deepen to brick-red. 'What do you think, Jan?'

'They *have* been looking forward to it — the safari park.'

'No one told me.' Sid took a map from a sideboard drawer and checked the route. 'Well,' he conceded, 'it's not too long or difficult a drive. You really want to go there?'

Darren nodded vigorously then, realizing that his father wasn't looking at him, said, 'There are lions and tigers and monkeys and they come right up to the car and there are game-wardens with guns in case anyone gets out of the car when they shouldn't. And a fair, too. And there are places for picnics.'

Jan could see that the issue was decided. She went to the kitchen to make sandwiches.

They ate the picnic in the car, misted-in, cramped, clammy and cold, watching the thin drizzle accrete to rivulets that wobbled unevenly down the windows and clung to the rubber beading in shimmering lines. A wind gusted across the open spaces of the safari park, rocking the car from time to time and whinnying when it struck a door-join or the baffle of an air vent. The interior of the car had a faint smell of damp dog mixed with the pungency of stale smoke and the blackened ends of aged cigarette butts.

A glistening worm of tomato pulp and seeds slithered down Nickie's forearm, puddled in the crook of his elbow, then slopped — a viscous gobbet — into Sid's lap. He snatched a tissue from the box on Jan's lap and wiped ineffectually. Nickie crushed the rest of the tomato with his fat little fist, watching the juice and seeds dribble down; the mess went somewhere out of sight: somewhere beyond Sid's knees but — he felt sure — well short of his shoes.

'For God's sake!' He lifted the child off his lap and handed him to Jan, who prised the mashed tomato away from him. Nickie began to cry, an ill-tempered, hoarse yowl that couldn't be reasoned with. From the back seat there came a sharp yell, followed by some scuffling that made the car wallow from side to side.

'Oh, for God's sake!' Sid repeated. 'Behave yourselves, both of you,' and he swiped a blow at Darren, catching him harder than he had meant and provoking tearful screams of pain and outrage.

'I didn't do anything. It was Geoff. He took the last cheese roll. I didn't do *anything*!' Darren aimed a punch at his brother, who ducked sideways and slammed into the front passenger-seat, nudging Jan forward so that she slopped hot coffee on to her dress and on to Nickie's leg. Nickie went rigid with pain. His mouth opened so wide that it seemed the jaws would separate; his face went purple; his body arched. There was a silence, for about three or four seconds, that resembled the silence after an echo has finally faded – particularly eerie, though, in that it seemed to be accruing a sound rather than shedding it. The scream flowed in and strengthened, grew until it seemed that the piercing pitch and strength would last forever; then Nickie's breath caught and the noise fell away for a moment until he filled his lungs once more and a second, identical, shriek followed the first.

Sid got out of the car and stood in the rain. He slammed the door, walked a little way off and stopped. Then he circled the car until he was behind it and some thirty feet back and stood in the rain without moving for five minutes, swearing under his breath every foul word he could think of and then using some of them over again.

They had hit bad traffic on the motorway after about forty-five miles: a tail-back resulting from the lanes being reduced from three to one. After a few miles of nose-to-tail driving, the kids – especially Nickie – had become fractious. Three times, Sid had been forced to pull over on to the hard shoulder after urgent cries of 'Wees, Mummy' from the toddler. On each occasion, he had eased back out into the slow-moving traffic to a cacophony of angry horn-blasts. As they had trickled on, a wafting layer of exhaust gases which lay beneath the mist of rain had seeped into the vehicles. Darren had begun to feel sick. Then Darren *was* sick. Sid had pulled over on to the hard shoulder again.

Once inside the safari park, they had made straight for the picnic area. Darren no longer felt ill; he felt better and hungry and thirsty. The drizzle had thickened, washing the colour out of fields and buildings. The funfair was deserted: unlit, unmanned, silent. The picnic area was crammed with cars, each with its windows fogged by breath and pearled with the thin rain. Inside each, dim shapes heaved to and fro – elbows and bobbing heads, arms stretching back and

forth with Thermos flasks and plastic bowls of unmanage-
able, sticky foodstuffs. Sid alone stood in the open air,
swearing, as the rainwater seeped under his collar.

Fifty yards away, alongside the park's principal road, was
a restaurant. It occurred to Sid that the restaurant was
almost certain to have a bar: and within a minute or two of
thinking that, he was in the place and downing his first
whisky. After the third, some of the chill and misery left
him. After the fourth, he bought a half-bottle to take with
him, then wandered, a little uncertainly, back to the car.

He eased himself into the driver's seat and slammed the
car door. No one spoke. The children looked sullen. Jan
stared straight ahead through the windscreen. She didn't
actually move, though it seemed to Sid as though her entire
right side had shrunk from him as he sat down. It was the
kind of silence that drills holes in granite. He took a sip from
his bottle, then wedged it between dashboard and windscreen: a pleasingly ambiguous gesture, since it combined
possible defiance with an apparent willingness to share.

'Well.' He tried a smile but got no response. 'Well − I
suppose we'd better go and look at the bloody animals.'

On the mesh of the enclosure's fence, a notice warned
visitors that they shouldn't leave their cars, wind down
their windows or feed the animals, that if they broke down
they should sound their horns and sit tight, that no responsibility was taken for any damage that might be done to any
vehicles. A pompous paunch in crisp khaki approached the
car window, then sank from sight − replaced by a red face
topped by a green beret.

'Read the notice?'

'Yes.' Sid nodded.

The paunch heaved back into view and a beefy hand
waved them through into the enclosure. They drove for ten
minutes without seeing anything at all. The rain began to
quicken, coming across the park in gusty grey squalls that
rapped sharply on the car roof, then settled into a steady,

dark, drumming downpour.

'I think there's something over there.' Darren pointed off to the left. 'I think it's a lion. It might be two lions.'

'It's a log,' Geoff said haughtily.

'It was a lion,' Darren insisted, staring through the back window, 'I think it was. Mummy, can you see anything?'

Jan didn't speak, she hadn't spoken for fifteen minutes or so. Darren switched his attention to his father. 'Can you see anything, Dad?'

Sid uncapped the bottle, took a swig, restored it to the dashboard.

'Darren,' he replied wearily, 'I can barely see the bonnet of the car. However, so far as I can judge, the Home Counties' version of the Serengeti is not remarkable for its abundance of exotic wildlife. Its verdant grasslands are not, so far as I can discern, teeming with herds of this, prides of that, or flocks of the other. Nowhere does the lithe, fierce predator descend on to the sleek back of his prey to rend him fang and nail. Whither — and well may you ask — the sly hyena chortling over the strewn and gory entrails of a kill; where the sound of thunder from ten thousand trampling hooves and the bowel-emptying roar of the rogue male? It strikes me, too, that this bit of the Great Plains seems to get a rather disproportionate amount of rain, don't you agree? We might spot a dolphin or two before we leave.'

'You're pissed,' said Jan, still looking straight ahead. Sid turned and sneered at her; they were rounding a slight bend; when he looked back at the road, they were within ten feet of a full-grown bull elephant. He applied the brakes. When people picked themselves up from the floor and generally disentangled, they were within several inches of a full-grown bull elephant. It was very big and utterly immobile. It looked at Sid, who looked back at it, through the hanging curtain of rain. Sid took another small drink. 'Lo!' he declaimed triumphantly. 'An elephant.'

They sat for five minutes or so, watching the elephant do nothing. The elephant then did nothing for a further five minutes while cars piled up behind Sid's.

Darren said: 'Drive round it, Daddy?'

Geoff said: 'Why won't it move?'

Jan said: 'For God's sake, Sid, we'll be here all day.'

Someone four or five cars back blew his horn.

Nickie said: 'Wees, Mummy, *wees*.'

Carefully, Sid engaged first gear. With pinpoint precision, he steered a line equidistant from the elephant and the edge of the road. Chummily, almost, the elephant sidestepped, as if reluctant to see them go. Sid clapped a hand to the horn. It's difficult to say whether the elephant was scared, affronted, startled or confused. Probably one of these. In any case, it kicked Sid's car.

Few car manufacturers, when deciding on the specifications for a new model to attract the punter and make obsolete last year's design, allow for a contingency of quite that sort. Rough roads, heavy rain, braking distances, cubic feet of storage space, those kinds of thing are considered, weighed, decided upon. Kicks from elephants are not the sort of hazard that tends to occur to the average manufacturer when conferring with his designers. It's not one of the brochure's principal selling-points. Just as well, by and large, since a kick from an elephant will dent your bodywork every time. It dented Sid's. In fact, his door caved in.

Sid gunned the car on to the grass, gouging a neat pair of tyre-tracks before finding purchase on the road again. Then he drove at an illegal speed to the other side of the enclosure, barrelled through the exit gate and screeched to a halt by the warden's hut. He wrenched at the buckled door, but it was irrevocably wedged.

'You'll have to get out.'

Jan opened the door and went to find a lavatory for Nickie. She and Darren and Geoff had attempted to remark on the incident during the breakneck ride through the en-

87

closure, but hadn't been able to interrupt the slow, steady rhythm of Sid's cursing. He became even more inventive as he rounded the car and inspected the damage.

The door was creased into a wedge-shape. The panel immediately behind it was crumpled like tin-foil. Both windows were cracked. The wing bore a long, shallow dent that ran almost to the headlight. The warden joined Sid and they stood in the sluicing rain and looked at the damage together.

'One of your bloody elephants,' Sid told him.

'Really?' The warden seemed less interested in the stove-in bodywork than the ability of an elephant to produce such an effect. 'Which one?' he asked. Sid looked at him. There was a homicidal glint in his eye which the warden seemed not to detect. 'Big grey bugger. Trunk, small tail, vestigial tusks, wrinkled skin, stumpy sort of feet. What the hell do you mean − which one? The one that kicks cars. That one.'

The warden thought he saw the joke. He laughed. 'Bad luck, squire. They can be funny, though; unpredictable, elephants. Bad luck.'

'Bad luck, nothing.' Sid flicked rainwater from his hair. 'What are you going to do about it?'

'Nothing that can be done, old cock. Own risk. You saw the notice, didn't you? Own risk, you see.'

'What's he saying?' Jan had deposited Nickie in the car and joined her husband.

'So far as I can gather,' Sid remarked with deceptive casualness, 'he appears to be telling me that we can't hold the safari park responsible for the fact that one of their elephants has reduced the car to scrap metal. So far as I can gather.'

'Own risk.' The warden nodded, glad that Sid seemed to have taken the point. As they left the park, Sid remarked that it hadn't been a wholly successful day − had it? − and he finished the last of the whisky and chucked the bottle out of Jan's window, since his wouldn't open at all.

It was small compensation that the traffic seemed to be flowing freely on the return journey: no orange-and-white cones, no absent workmen who had deserted their generators. Sid was more than anxious to get home; everyone was; and despite the damage to the car, it was clocking ninety without effort.

After twenty miles or so, the rain let up. The motorway was blotched with damp and drying patches. Sid reckoned that, sooner or later, Jan would try to say something consolatory, so he uttered what he intended to be his only remark of the return trip: 'Don't say *anything*: O.K.?'

Jan didn't speak, Darren did. It was a silly thing to say. He said: 'I wish we'd gone to the pictures.'

Sid missed him with the first swipe — turning in his seat to get the blow in — so he tried again with the backhander. The boy ducked professionally. The car swerved from the outer lane to the middle. 'Sid! Christ!' Jan clutched Nickie closer. 'Sid, for Christ's sake!'

He corrected the drift, noticing that the car behind him flashed its lights; then it came round on his near-side and kept pace. He glanced over and looked away. When he glanced over again, it was with more concern. The policeman was flagging him, with an extended arm from the open window. Sid braked, fell back, crossed two lanes to the hard shoulder and pulled up. The police car stopped just ahead of him; both doors opened, both policemen got out and closed on him. He tried to wind the window down, but it was stuck.

'Wind your window . . . oh,' he stopped short. Jan had already lowered the window on her side. A head poked in. 'Could you wind your window down, please, sir?' The voice was polite in the way that executioners are said to be polite.

'Ah — like to,' Sid smiled. 'It won't, though.'

'Get out of the car, please.'

'Like to — can't. The door's jammed.'

89

'Don't bugger me about, mate,' said the policeman. 'Get out of the sodding car.'

Jan got out, taking Nickie with her. Sid shuffled across her seat and got out too. Then she got back in, leaving him to it. The policemen strolled round the car, observing carefully. Then they confronted Sid.

'Driving at an average of ninety miles an hour. We clocked you. Driving erratically, too.'

'Surely not?' Sid smiled. 'Just taking the family home.'

'I see.' The policeman whose head had first appeared at Jan's window went back to the car's off-side and looked at the buckled metalwork. 'Been in an accident have we?' he wanted to know.

'No. Well, yes. No, not an accident *as such*,' Sid offered.

'How did you get that lot, then? It's new damage, isn't it?'

'Yes; yes it is; it's new. Yes. It wasn't an accident, though. Not as such.' Sid grinned suicidally.

'Perhaps you'd better tell us how it happened,' said one of them.

'How did it happen?' demanded the other.

Sid looked from one to the other. They waited. He chuckled. He said: 'It was kicked in by an elephant.' They waited. He said, 'I met an elephant on the road and it kicked the car in.'

They chuckled. One of them went to get the breathalyser bag. The other said: 'You're sure you weren't attacked by King Kong, mate?'

The crystals were greener than grass when he blew into the tube. They arrested him and left Jan and the three kids to wait for a tow-truck — in the rain, on the hard shoulder. They waited for forty minutes. Nickie said, 'Wees, Mummy.'

The Bite

Being the wife of a diplomat doesn't usually make for a particularly easy life: the social round might look glamorous from a distance, but it involves a good deal of hard work, careful organization and saintly forbearance, under the best of circumstances. Things are made a lot more difficult, though, in the less salubrious foreign postings. To be 'an embassy wife' in New York, or Vienna or Rome can make life more pleasant and interesting than it otherwise might be; other postings are not nearly so diverting.

Sheila Burton's husband was an Under-Secretary in an African country fabled for its lack of the common comforts. The temperature rarely dropped below the mid-90°s, the humidity was close to 100 per cent, fungus grew on clothes if they were left in cupboards for any length of time, water had to be boiled *and* purified . . . and in addition to all that, the natives were distinctly unfriendly.

For a year or more, Sheila had coped with rotting fabrics, incipient dysentery, aggressive servants and unbearable heat. Now she had had enough. She wanted to get back to England for a break. 'Just a month or so,' she told her husband, James. 'I want to feel a cold wind, and shop in a store, not a native street market, and drink a glass of water that hasn't been boiled ten times, and . . . '

James was an understanding man; he could see that nothing could be gained — though much could be lost — by insisting that she stay by his side. A rest would probably make all the difference. He agreed that she should return to England for the month of April; but first they would take a short holiday together: four days or so up-country, to relax and be in each other's company before their separation.

Though she had come to hate the country, Sheila enjoyed their little holiday. Roughing it (which meant staying in what passed for hotels and having to eat food she hadn't selected and prepared herself) didn't seem too bad with the prospect of a return to England to look forward to. As she and James drove through the hot, harsh landscapes in pursuit of wildlife and strange sights, she often allowed her thoughts to go ahead of her to England: to reunions, green fields, cool rain, a civilized life-style.

It was on the day before their journey back to the capital that a tiny moment of drama occurred. They had taken the Land Rover into the bush — not far, but far enough to be able to focus a zoom lens on a herd of baboons — and had found some shade under a small tree where they could enjoy their Thermos flask of vodka martinis, enthusiastically (but badly) mixed by the barman at their hotel. They had been sipping for five minutes or so when Sheila suddenly squealed and leapt to her feet, slapping madly at the side of her neck.

'What was it?' James jumped up too.

'A spider. Must have dropped out of the tree. It bit me.' She was looking at the ground about her; and after a couple of seconds James spotted the creature, lying where it had fallen, stunned by Sheila's blow. It was bright red and had a rather fat body, but wasn't particularly large or repulsive; even so, he shuddered as he crushed it with his boot.

'Let's take a look.'

Sheila showed him the place on her neck, just below the

ear, where she had felt the nip.

'Doesn't look bad,' he reassured her. 'In fact it's barely visible. Just the same, we'll get it treated. I don't think there are any poisonous spiders that look quite like that. But let's get back to the hotel.'

When they returned, James tried to locate a doctor. The hotel staff couldn't help him (it seemed, in his experience, they never could) and there was no one he knew in the area to whom to appeal for information. He was a little worried but Sheila's initial alarm had faded.

'After all,' she reasoned, 'if it had been poisonous, then presumably I'd be dead by now.' At the back of her mind was the fear that if she were put 'under observation' or if the incident were officially reported, her trip to England might have to be postponed. In any case, she felt fine. Even common English harvest-spiders nipped, she knew that. She put the whole thing out of her mind and James, it appears, did the same.

The first few days of her return to England were crowded, happy and exciting. She shopped, saw her family and friends, went to the theatre, ate food that tasted like ambrosia and took delight in the cold English spring weather. She was making-up one morning before going out to enjoy a stroll in the park when she noticed the small red swelling on her neck. She remembered the spider and was faintly concerned. The bump was really not much, though, and she was determined simply to ignore it, assuming it would go away. Some sort of delayed reaction, she thought; if anything serious had been going to happen, she would have known days before.

It did not go away, though. Each day, she examined the lump in her mirror — and each day it had swollen a little more and seemed more inflamed. Obviously, it was a localized infection, although it was pulpy — soft — to the touch, not hard like a boil. Finally, she decided to go to a doctor.

The G.P. didn't seem too worried. He agreed that it was

an infection, and listened with some interest to the story of the spider, but reassured her that it wasn't causing any glandular swelling, or spreading at all, so would certainly disappear soon. He prescribed some penicillin and sent her away.

Five days later, the swelling was very noticeable, though still not painful. It made her neck look misshapen and she was self-conscious about it. More than that, it seemed to move when she pressed at it, as if it were not rooted; and the feeling made her skin prickle with mild revulsion.

Over the next two or three days it grew even bigger. It troubled her to the extent that she wouldn't go out — except to see the doctor again, who showed no more concern than on her first visit but took the precaution of writing a prescription for more antibiotics. That same evening, she cancelled a dinner date and stayed in. She watched television and cooked scrambled eggs for herself. At about ten-thirty she decided to have a bath and go to bed.

The bath-water was almost injuriously hot: the way she liked it. She lowered herself in, sank back, and allowed the water to creep up her body until only her head and neck were above the surface. For ten minutes or so she soaked like that, adding more scaldingly hot water from time to time, luxuriating in the heat and steam. Then she felt a pop — accompanied by a sharp sensation like the sting of a plucked hair — on her neck where the swelling was. Surprised, she sat up, and turned towards the mirror-tiles that bordered the bath, to see what had happened.

At that point she started to scream, churning the bath-water, threshing to get out, swatting hysterically about her face with her hands like someone fending off a demon.

Running down her shoulder and upper arm, tumbling on to her breast, swarming into her hair and on to her face, scattering on to the sides of the bath and into the water — pouring like a vile cataract from the open wound in her neck — were dozen upon dozen of tiny red spiders.

A Last Fling

It was Friday. Janet knew it was Friday because the alarm clock hadn't woken her: she hadn't set it the night before. Not that she usually slept in on Fridays. Under normal circumstances she would have been sitting at her office desk for more than two hours. This Friday was special because it was the Friday preceding the Saturday on which she would be married and the day had been set aside for what her mother referred to as 'last-minute preparations'.

For the life of her, Janet couldn't imagine what *they* might be. So far as she could judge, everything had been ready for a month or more: dress purchased, cake made, invitations issued, flowers and cars ordered, church and restaurant booked, honeymoon arrangements finalized . . . Her mother had revelled in it all, becoming bossy and hysterical by turns, but secretly enjoying every second.

All in all, Janet was fed up to the back teeth with the wedding. She hated the prospect of being the centre of gloating attention. Hated, too, the business of meeting all those strangers: Duncan's relatives, his friends (the best man was a colleague from his office who sounded horribly pompous and boringly ambitious), relatives of her own whom she hadn't seen since she was a girl — all playing the part of bosom friends or favourite aunts or roguish uncles. She felt rather as if she were being prepared for a ritual sacrifice — rather like the king-for-a-day of legend, who enjoyed a brief time of complete indulgence only to be offered to the harvest gods after his short reign was over. There was a deeper irritation, though, behind her impatience with the fussing, the clucking, the intermittent tears and the endless practical details. It had to do with the fact that she didn't really want to marry at all. She didn't want to be a wife, didn't want to be tied to a permanent partner, didn't want her freedom and independence to end. Sometimes, she even allowed these thoughts into her conscious brain, although most of the time she repressed them. If she had been entirely honest with herself, she would have had to admit that she didn't really want Duncan either.

Duncan was eminently suitable; at least he suited her mother and father and that was what mattered most, it seemed. Janet knew, of course, that she would have to get married sooner or later. Girls from her social background usually did. Parents worried about a single daughter over twenty-five; and they fretted about having no grandchildren. There was always an example of marital virtue to be referred to, always the notion of security to be insisted upon. Duncan had started out as a series of casual dates, had then become a 'steady', and at some stage had been seized on by her parents as the perfect husband. Since Duncan had been as keen on the idea as Janet's parents, she had been (or so it had appeared to her) powerless to resist. After six proposals rejected, she finally gave in out of sheer battle-fatigue.

She had consoled herself, since then, with the notion that she could have done much worse. He was well-off, was clearly set for a successful career as a merchant banker, her friends thought him attractive; in addition to that he was a competent lover, indulged her most of the time, was thoughtful and — not unimportant — easy to control.

He was also inexpressibly dull. It was a fact that, until now, Janet had preferred not to admit to herself; but with the wedding only one day away, it was something that couldn't easily be denied. She was headed for a life of secure, well-to-do boredom. Tedious dinner parties, cocktail parties in the city, routine visits to tiresome West End plays, civilized weekends with Duncan's parents or her own which would entail sherry, bridge, walks with the dogs and polite chit-chat. She could see her life leaking away.

For the rest of that day, she got through the tidying-up of arrangements. She had morning coffee with her mother, who seemed eager to find something disastrously left undone: there was nothing of course. Her lunch date was with an old friend, a girl who had been married only two months before and was still as enthusiastic about the business as she had been for the two months preceding the wedding. Babies were next on her agenda and she spent most of the lunch telling Janet — rather avidly — how the planning for this event was to be arranged. Janet thought the whole thing sounded rather impersonal — rather like a merger or the production of a new strain of hybrid rose.

She spent the late afternoon and early evening alone in her flat, sipping gin and tonic and making a half-hearted attempt to sort out the books, clothes, records and so forth that she would want to transfer to Duncan's flat when they returned from their honeymoon. She had made it clear that there was to be no hen-party; the idea appalled her; and, in any case, she had known that one day of crowing and crooning from her friends was as much as she could take.

As the evening wore on, though, she began to feel restless. Without quite knowing what she might do, or where she might go, she left the flat, got into her car and drove off — aimlessly at first, but after a time the car seemed to almost point itself in the direction of Hampstead. In her student days, she had spent a lot of time, with friends, drinking in a

97

pub near Hampstead pond. She had shared a small house with six or seven other people in their late teens or early twenties: a house full of music, booze, dramatic rows and crazy happenings. It would be good, she thought, to revisit a place where she had once been happy and irresponsible – and unattached.

The pub hadn't changed much: which surprised her and, because it looked so familiar, depressed her too. It served to remind her of the time when she had been fancy-free. She sat at the bar, ordered a drink and looked around. Sitting at the curve of the bar was a young man – thirty or so, she guessed, and good-looking. She allowed her glance to linger a moment, then saw that he was gazing back at her. She looked away, faintly embarrassed; then curiosity compelled her to look his way again. He was still watching her, smiling slightly. 'Good Lord,' she thought, 'I'm being picked up.'

At first, the idea simply amused her. Then it began to interest her. She had drunk enough to be feeling slightly reckless; and the prospect of tomorrow's ceremony and the life that would follow it strengthened the effect of the gin. 'Why not,' she mused. 'A last fling.' It seemed a suitably rebellious idea. Her own secret; something a bit outrageous. A one-night stand the night before her wedding!

She felt the man still looking at her. When she next looked up, she returned the gaze steadily and smiled. Then, pausing just long enough for dramatic effect, finished her drink and walked along the bar to where he sat. 'Hullo,' he said; and waited.

'It'll have to be your place,' she told him.

'Very direct and to the point.'

She smiled. 'I'm not a whore . . . '

'I didn't think you were,' he interrupted.

' . . . but I'm right about what you were thinking?'

'Oh, yes.'

'Fine. Two things you have to understand: no names; and

nothing after tonight.'

'An adventure!' he laughed. 'Sounds terrific.'

They exchanged no more than a dozen words on the way to his flat — a basement some ten minutes' walk away. After he had closed the door they stood and looked at each other for a minute, then he led the way to the bedroom. Janet kicked her shoes off. 'This is the end of an era,' she remarked wryly.

'Mysterious,' he said. 'Let's go to bed.'

He was good — really very good; and she was rapacious. They made love lengthily, inventively, four times. For the most part, what they said to each other was instructional; little was said in the moments between love-making. They did things to each other that surprised both of them, but delighted them too. Then, at three-thirty in the morning, Janet said, 'I must go.' Without bothering to wait for his reply, she put on her clothes over the perspiration and the subtle odours and made to leave. He dragged a sheet round his body and came to the front door with her where, to his mild surprise, she kissed him warmly.

'Really — no names?' he asked.

'No names, no telephone numbers, no future.' She grinned at him. 'It was *very* nice. Goodbye.' He smiled back, raised a hand in a mock wave and shut the door.

A friend telephoned her the next morning, as arranged: which was just as well, or she might not have woken before noon. She lay in her bath, feeling rather smug and quite without any kind of remorse. She was, in fact, rather pleased with herself. She still felt that way later in the day when, with all the fuss and arrangements over, she walked down the aisle on her father's arm. 'I'm like the June bride,' she thought, remembering the old joke: 'sore but satisfied. Except I managed to feel that way *before* the ceremony!'

The idea made her smile, and the smile was still there when Duncan turned to greet her as she approached the altar. The best man turned, too; and Janet had time to register his stricken face before an awful mixture of panic and disbelief rose in her. She was wrong to have thought that the best man was someone she wouldn't know. In fact, she had got out of his bed only a few hours before!

In Jest

'What's her name?' Robert Fairfax asked the question without taking his eyes from her.

'Leonora Harris.'

'Leonora? I don't believe you.'

'Fine. Don't.' Max Saunders, like his friend, was looking at the girl. They stood side by side in the doorway, speaking to one another but looking clear across the room, through the partial screen of drinkers and dancers, to where Leonora Harris was sitting. Her long legs were stretched out on the floor and she had put a cushion between her head and the wall. She was directly underneath a standard lamp and very close to one of the speakers. A man was kneeling at her feet like a supplicant, trying to make some headway with whatever line he had devised; he squinted against the glare from the lamp (kneeling there put him a level lower than the lampshade) and tried to make the most of the few seconds of silence between tracks. Her eyes, for the most part, were half-closed. Her only concession to the man's address was to raise her eyelids slightly from time to time.

'Leonora?'

'Indeed, Leonora,' Max said. 'How could I have made up a name like that?'

'She's stunning.'

'Verily, she is stunning.' Max sighed. 'She is also un-available.'

'Are you sure? Married or something?'

'No, not married; not something. No ties, no let or hin-drance — also no inclination, or so it seems!'

Robert looked at his friend in astonishment — most of it real. 'You don't mean to say that she doesn't!'

'So far as one can gather — from talking to others and, sadly, from one's own recent experience — that would appear to be the case, yes. She doesn't go out with blokes, doesn't accept invitations to subtly candle-lit dinners *à deux*, doesn't fall prey to the wiles of handsome types like you and me, doesn't pair off at parties, or team up at teas. Doesn't. Sad, isn't it?'

'It's appalling. She's beautiful.'

'Rob, I understand just what you mean by the juxta-positioning of those two statements, but it's not logical. It ought to be, but it's not. I shall re-charge my goblet with the unspeakable plonk our host is serving and attempt to stalk some game that's rather more game, if you see what I mean.' He pushed himself away from the door jamb. 'In fact, I think I'll try to get down-wind of that little blonde by the window. I'm reliably informed that she's not at all averse to bearing the White Man's Burden.'

Rob chuckled and waved his friend off. He kept his eyes fixed on Leonora, though. Apart from the fact that she really was very beautiful indeed, she now seemed some-thing of an oddity. When he and Max had first become medical students, they had reasoned that they could count on two constant factors: a grant and available women. Nor had they been disappointed. The government had stumped up and the girls, by and large, had come across. One other constant factor was hard work, but neither of them minded that. They liked to let their hair down at parties like to-night's and were not wholly opposed to spending an occasional evening in the pub, but their days — and many of their nights — were long and demanding. Both Robert and Max worked diligently to succeed; between times, they liked to have fun.

The supplicant had given up. Rob watched her and wondered whether she was conscious of his interest. He decided that she was. He also decided to leave her alone: tonight, he would do nothing. If she knew that he had been looking at her, then she would be expecting him to go across, talk to her, try to get her interested. He wouldn't do that. But he would do a little investigating to make sure that she didn't go out of his life for too long.

The party, as parties will, began to come apart at the seams. The booze was almost finished, a few people had gone to sleep in various parts of the house, the dancers began to thin out and cars were starting up in the road outside. Rob waited until he was pretty sure that Leonora's attention was engaged elsewhere, then slipped out of the room: a mysterious exit, he felt; something to keep her guessing. He drove slowly back to the flat he shared with Max, thinking about her, slightly annoyed that she already seemed to have a slight advantage over him, slightly intrigued that the annoyance could exist.

When he got in, he discovered Max slumped in one of their battered armchairs, sipping a whisky. He raised the glass. 'Needed this to get the taste of that foul Bulgarian wine off my palate.'

Rob took off his coat and sat in the other chair. 'The little blonde, I imagine, caught your scent and took off across the veldt. It's the repellent aftershave you wear.'

'Almost right,' Max smiled ruefully. 'Her beau caught my scent. Charmless bloke — six foot four with muscles like a coal-heaver and fingers like bunches of bananas, so he's probably all set to be a brain surgeon. He offered to eviscerate me one-handed. I scarred him with the sharp edge of my tongue and left with my dignity intact.'

'What?'

'Called him a dirty name and ran for it.'

'Yes.' Rob got up and fetched himself a whisky. 'Tell me', he said, 'about Leonora.'

'Aha!' Max grinned. 'On the hook, are we?'

'Not at all.' Rob paused. 'Though I confess that I'm drawn to the bait. Who is she?'

'Leonora Harris. Works somewhere in the town . . . solicitor's office, I think, or maybe it's an estate agent's, I'm not sure. She's a friend of one of the nurses — Sheila what'sit, the redhead. She comes to a party now and then — not often — and invariably drives every red-blooded male in the place half-crazy with desire. I've only seen her once before — that rather tiresome bash you missed three weeks ago. Tried, failed, asked questions, was told what I told you earlier by a number of lovelorn types and, like the practical chap I am, decided to put her out of mind. Not an easy task. Interesting . . . ' He got up for the whisky bottle.

'What's interesting?' Rob wanted to know.

'It seems she's a little *weird*. Or so people say . . . have said.'

'How weird? I mean, in what way?'

'Well, to begin with, she's one of those brown rice and fennel freaks. Not just a vegetarian, she only eats vegetables and suchlike: no fish or eggs or whatever.'

'Not so weird, really.'

'No, that's not all — or it's the least of it. She's got this odd . . . *thing* . . . about silence. According to Sheila what's-her-name, Leonora likes to spend speechless weeks. For a whole week, she refuses to speak at all; or make any kind of noise. Mostly, she just stays in her room, but if she can be tempted out, or goes somewhere, she simply refuses to talk or respond to anything. She even gets upset if she sneezes.'

'A religious thing?'

'No, I don't think so; I don't know really. No one seems to. It must be a bit eerie, though, don't you think?'

Rob nodded. 'I concede that it's strange to find a rivetingly lovely girl acting like a trainee Franciscan. Mysterious – not unattractive, if you see what I mean. Maybe it's all part of some clever technique. She did seem a little otherworldly this evening, though; genuine, not affected.'

'There's more.'

'There's more?'

'There's more. Sheila Thingy reports that our mysterygirl is given to bouts of what she describes as "uncontrollable hysteria". No one quite seems to know what sparks her off: something someone says, perhaps, but it's difficult afterwards to work out what it might have been; or something that's on TV . . . anyway, she takes off into her room, sometimes, and can be heard raving and yelling and crying and chucking things about; then she emerges, calm and seemingly O.K., but will probably go into one of her no-speak weeks. Never does it in public. The first few times, Sheila tried to go in to help her: thought the girl was having a fit or something. The door was locked and she considered calling for help, but in the end just waited it out. Whereupon, Leonora reappeared, unspeaking but collected. I think the other girls in their flat have got used to it by now.'

'O.K., that's weird.'

'That's what I thought.'

'But it won't stop me trying to see her.'

Max smiled at his friend. 'No,' he said, 'I didn't think it would.'

Rob's first move was to get Leonora's address and send her flowers – no note, just a large bunch of lilies delivered by Interflora. Anonymous lilies; it had occurred to Rob that he could devise mysteries of his own. His next piece of strategy involved sending unsigned messages to her office – it *was* a solicitor's, he discovered that easily enough – so that she would open them with her morning mail. Each message took the form of a text reference, just that. The Song of Solomon, Omar Khayyám, the Romantic poets, bits of *Wuthering Heights*: his choice was limited by his sparse reading, so eventually he took to using a Dictionary of Quotations. Lilies twice a week, but unpredictably spaced – sometimes he organized them to be almost a full week apart, sometimes he sent them on consecutive days – references to some apposite work of literature each day: he followed the routine for a month and, during that time, saw Leonora only twice. The first time was by chance at a party when, using a determined logistical device, he managed to avoid her completely while still being able to observe her. That was good for his plan, but bad for his psyche; the effort of not being near her stung him and provoked him to drive to her flat a few days later and sit outside in the car to watch her return from work. He stayed in the car for a very long time, waiting to see if she would come out again, or whether he might catch a glimpse of her at a window. She didn't; he didn't. It stung him more acutely.

Finally, he decided that the moment had arrived to announce himself as her anonymous suitor. She must, he reasoned, be intrigued by this time and, in any case, his deliberate restraint – whether or not it had had an effect on her – had brought him to a strange state of feverish impatience. In effect, he had taken the hook and thrust it through his own lip. One evening, he waited in his car until she arrived home. After the door had closed behind her, he let five minutes elapse then, taking a bunch of lilies from the back seat, crossed the road to her flat and rang the bell. The door opened instantly. He offered the flowers and she took them, saying nothing, waiting for him to act or speak. She stood in the doorway, obliging him to remain on the pavement.

'I'm Robert Fairfax.' He made an attempt at a little courtly bow, but before he had completed the gesture he knew it to be awkward and ridiculous. He straightened up, clumsily, feeling a flush of embarrassment tingling in his cheeks.

'I've been sending . . .' He half-raised a hand to indicate the lilies. ' . . . and I'm your mystery correspondent. The little texts,' he went on needlessly.

'Yes.' She stood with the lilies in the crook of her arm, the blooms lying on her right shoulder, the broad, ribbed leaves brushing the soft sweep of her hair. She was lovelier than any girl he had ever seen; her beauty was definable, absolute, it seemed. She didn't so much possess beauty as embody it. 'Yes, I know who you are.' Her voice was oddly haughty, but not harsh.

'You might have seen me at a few parties. I've certainly seen you.' He smiled, getting nothing back. Her eyes were completely devoid of curiosity: a touch of anger, perhaps, nothing else.

'Well,' he tried, 'at least you're speaking to me. I gather,' he tried to cover the mistake, 'I gather you're not always terribly talkative. Look, could I come in, perhaps, or maybe you'd like to come out? We could have a drink and go for a meal. Interested?' It was too late for the casual approach, he knew, but there wasn't much left for him.

'Just a minute.' She half-closed the door, leaving him outside, and went upstairs. 'For her coat,' he reasoned and smiled to himself. He had succeeded — at least to some degree — where others had failed. Maybe he had detected a touch of anger in her look; that was all right — the flowers, the texts, the whole campaign had put her in a position where she owed him an evening of her company, if nothing else. He would work on it from there.

When she returned, she was carrying the flowers he had given her — all the flowers he had given her. She held them out and, in his bewilderment, he accepted them, holding his arms extended as if he were supporting a skein of wool. She placed an envelope edgewise on his left palm and he closed his index finger and thumb to trap it; then she turned and eased the door to with her back to him — an almost absent-minded motion, contemptuous in its casualness.

He stood in the street and looked at the flowers. More than half of them were shrivelled and brown; the rest − apart from those he had sent a few days before and the ones he had brought with him − had very little life left in them. None had even been put in water. The elastic bands still gripped the stalks as they would have done when the flower shop delivered them.

Humiliation rose as a cord of bile in his throat. He choked and wanted to spit, but swallowed instead as he walked back to his car and hurled the dead and dying lilies on to the back seat. He could feel people in the street watching him and quaked with a sudden anger that was built of rejection and tattered pride, together with a fierce sense of injustice and an understanding of his own mawkish stupidity.

Had the note referred him − as his notes had referred her − to some suitable text, had she, even in that small way, entered the spirit of his wooing or offered the tiniest flattery by copying his style, had she pointed towards some text that made mention of solitariness or doomed love, then, perhaps, his outrage might have been less. As it was, the note simply read: *I would be grateful if you would stop annoying me.* The terseness of it, and the pomposity, the mound of dead flowers on the back seat of his car, the way she had closed the door without even bothering to look at him, turned his embarrassment to fury. He gripped the steering-wheel, twisting his hands as if trying to snap it in two, shoulders hunched, arms rigid and trembling with tension. Then he let his breath out in a rush, leaning forward so that his forehead rested against the rim of the wheel, and said, 'You bloody fool, Fairfax.' After that he drove home, slowly, thinking.

'Very much to the point, isn't it?' Max was holding the note in one hand, a drink in the other. 'Not a great effort to let you down lightly.'

'You spotted that, did you?' Rob smiled. 'Yes, you could

say it was on the brusque side of considerate. What's particularly galling is the amount of time, money and effort I expended on the wretched girl. Flowers costing the earth and a couple of hemispheres, midnight delvings into arcane quotations, plotting my plan of action in order to gain the element of surprise; I didn't even have the nervous energy left for other, easier, conquests.'

Max patted him on the back, consolingly, and handed him a glass. '*C'est la guerre,* old cock. Try to think of it as a poor investment; there's a lot of gilt-edged about.'

'It's O.K.,' Rob shrugged. 'I felt deeply stupid to begin with, I confess: standing there in the bloody street with my arms full of mummified flowers; the note didn't exactly make me feel rosy with well-being, either. I made the mistake of wanting something too much. You always run the risk of making a damn fool of yourself when you give in to that — want quickly becomes need becomes obsession. It's all right, though. She's beautiful beyond belief, but she's out of my system. Except . . . ' he smiled and took a sip of his drink, 'I don't believe I'm quite through with Miss Harris yet. Not quite.'

Max was interested. 'Meaning?'

'When are you next in the dissecting room, Max?'

'Tomorrow as it happens.'

'That's what I thought. Could you bring back a present for the herbivorous Leonora?'

'What had you in mind?'

Rob told him. 'And then,' he went on, 'maybe you could swing an invitation for the two of us to have a nightcap at Sheila the redhead's flat: after we've taken her and a friend out to dinner, naturally.'

'Shouldn't be a problem,' Max said. 'Rob . . . ' he hesitated. 'Look, why not just let it drop? You said you were over it now.'

'I am. But I do feel a parting gift would be in order.'

Max looked at him a moment, then started to laugh.

'You're a nut, you really are. All right, I'll do it; but if she goes through the roof, the responsibility's yours. You're a loony.' And he started to laugh again.

'You're going to do what?' Sheila pulled back her shaggy, red fringe the better to stare at Rob.

Rob told her again. 'I am going to put an amputated leg in Leonora's bed. Tucked up cosily — with the foot on the pillow, I thought that would be a nice touch.'

Janice, Rob's date for the evening, broke into startled laughter. Sheila persisted. 'Where is the bloody thing?'

'It's in the boot of the car; parcelled up neatly in newspaper. It's perfectly fresh — not at all whiffy.'

Sheila chuckled. 'Just because she gave you the elbow. You're barmy.'

Max agreed. 'That's what I told him. He's a determined lad, however, and not easily diverted from a plan once he's made his mind up to follow it through.'

'What do you want us to do?' Janice asked.

'Nothing,' said Rob, 'except keep quiet. Oh, you could smuggle in the lower limb if she happens to be in when we get back. Or lure her from her bedroom if she has already gone in there.'

'It's early,' remarked Sheila, 'only just past ten. She hardly ever goes to bed before midnight. Well,' she put on a formally polite smile, 'would you two young men care to join us for a drink or two at our bijou residence?'

They were chatting and playing music when Leonora arrived home — the four of them sprawled on the floor with a bottle of wine at hand. They looked up as she came into the room, watching for her reaction to Rob's presence. Somewhat to their disappointment she merely smiled — at Rob first, then at the rest of them.

'You'll understand if I don't join you,' she said.

'You have to admire her style,' thought Rob. 'If she's

under the impression that I'm dogging her, then she's refusing to give me the satisfaction of seeing that she's annoyed or put out; if she thinks I'm here to try to make her jealous by being with Janice, she's making it abundantly clear that she doesn't give a damn.' He smiled back and nodded at her, but didn't speak.

'Good night,' Sheila said, adding, 'sleep well.'

Leonora went into her room. For a moment, Rob experienced a fleeting regret — maybe the joke, his revenge, was going too far. Then he remembered how he had felt, laden with the flowers, clutching her supercilious note. Like the others, he waited for the scream, wondering whether he should be anticipating one of Leonora's notorious bouts of hysteria.

The scream never came. In fact, though they strained their ears for a sound, they could hear nothing at all. They looked at one another. 'She couldn't have missed it, I suppose?' asked Max.

'Not a chance,' Rob insisted. 'I left the foot in plain view — and the light on. She'd have to be blind not to see it.'

'She might have passed out,' Janice suggested. 'I might well have passed out myself and I'm a nurse — I've seen chopped-off bits and pieces before.'

Sheila got up. 'We'd better check,' she said. Together they tiptoed down the hallway to Leonora's room and stood outside the door. They listened; and, at first, failed to hear any noise. Then from inside the room came a faint sound, a sound that chilled them, though they couldn't identify it; or perhaps it was that, at first, their minds refused to identify it. They listened and heard it again — just audible, an odd, slobbering sound, a little, throaty *Mmmm Mmmm Mmmm* coming through the slobber, a pause, then a series of what sounded like tiny kisses. It came to them all in the same second. The realization came before Rob opened the door, before they saw what they knew they would see. The sounds they could hear were the sounds of someone eating.

111

Leonora looked up as they came into the room. Rob could see that she was mad: had become mad. The madness was in her eyes, in the animal-like pose as she stooped over the leg, trapping it on the bed with a hand clenched like a claw; the madness was in her slack, half-open mouth, dribbling the wet gobbets of flesh. She kept her head lowered, but watched them warily as she chewed.

The Escape

It was as if a searchlight had been brought to bear on the car: clicking on in the thick country darkness and flooding the interior with a steady pale glow, intense and deceptive like moonlight, shifting only when the car shifted – when he steered a curve in the narrow road – and seeming, then, to roll across the roof, down and across the facia, along his lap, over the passenger-seat and back to the roof; less troublesome for a moment but the source soon focusing again on his driving mirror, two hard discs of light bobbling there, thin shards radiating from the centre and threatening to blind him.

'Bloody fool!' Keith Jackson blipped his headlights three or four times in rapid succession and waited for the car behind him to dip its own, obediently. It didn't; in fact it drew a little closer to him, filling his mirror with brilliance, edge to edge. 'Idiot!' Keith snapped down the anti-glare switch just below the glass and the irritation sank back to a suffused smoky blur.

He had been on the road for better than five hours and still had an hour or more left to drive. He was tired. The rhythm had gone out of his handling, so that gear-changing and clutch work had become not quite automatic responses, a little ragged; and he was conscious of peering too carefully at roundabouts and junctions.

The four-day management course, which had ended at lunchtime with much jollity, shaking of hands, group photographs and promises to keep in touch, had been pretty demanding. Classes had started at nine a.m. and had often ended as late as ten p.m.; projects requiring research and the various skills of those in each group had been set for every one of the four days and had to be completed before pupils could slope off to the bar for a couple of stiff night-caps; and even then the talk tended to be about the work done that day — the lectures, the techniques. It was an oddly sequestered world. Everyone there had been sent — paid for — by his company and was expected to get the best out of it. Most were expected to write reports on their return. Keith had found the course stimulating and had worked hard. He wanted promotion and knew the course represented a rung or two on the ladder. But it had been wearying; and the drive back hadn't been easy: a long, dull motorway stretch, then heavy traffic on the trunk roads. A leaden edge of fatigue was on him, making him sluggish and clumsy. His head buzzed slightly, echoing the tingle in his fingers and feet; his eyes felt cold and swollen. The last thing he needed was an inconsiderate clot like the one behind him right now. The road was too narrow and had too many bends for overtaking. Although the headlights' glare wasn't troubling him any more, he was conscious of the other car all the time: nudging up behind him, deliber-ately coming too close, that arrogant full beam quite clearly saying, 'Get a move on.'

As a demonstration of his annoyance, Keith trod on the brake as he negotiated a slight bend. The following lights burgeoned mightily as the two cars came bonnet to boot, then fell away when the other driver braked responsively. The distance between them lengthened momentarily and Keith realized that the man behind must have had to reduce speed very sharply. He grinned, even though the lights swept up on him again.

As he came into the next short straight, Keith tapped the accelerator and put some distance between himself and his pursuer. Then, as he hit the crown of the bend, he changed down and dropped to half the speed he had been doing without having to apply the brake. As before, the lights washed over his upholstery and this time he heard a faint screech as his adversary's wheels locked for a second. Keith chuckled; but before he could gather speed and gain a new advantage, he saw the lights come up on his offside as the other car moved out to overtake. He slapped the accelerator pedal to the floor and felt the car buck. For a short time the two vehicles were side by side, jockeying for the lead; then a set of headlights appeared on the road ahead, illuminating the hedgerow and grass verge along the short approach to the bend Keith had just passed. It seemed as if the driver alongside Keith wasn't going to give way. He hung on until the very last. Then he braked violently, swerving and snaking to hold the road, before dropping back and hauling over to the left.

The oncoming car boomed by them and the road ahead was empty again. Keith watched the headlights come up fast in his wing mirror, ignoring the silver flood inside. He waited . . . waited . . . then jabbed down on the accelerator when the other man's bonnet nosed up to his offside door. This time, the other driver wasn't caught out. There was a roar as he dropped a gear and the next thing Keith saw was the dark smudge of a face staring at him as the cars drew level. They were no more than fifty metres from the next, tight, bend, but the other driver held his position. Instinctively, Keith slowed and braked; but there was no hope of letting the man in: he had to take the bend on the blind side, without the faintest notion of what might be opposing him. Without meaning to, or wanting to, he closed his eyes for the fraction of a second that it took for the other car to travel the bend. When he opened them, he was on the bend himself and moving too fast. He braked, tucked into the bend too steeply, corrected, then accelerated and steered out in time to see red tail-lights — intact and disappearing — on the road ahead. He breathed out for the first time in fifteen seconds, then found a sensible speed and held it.

'I'm as much of a fool as he is,' he thought ruefully. 'Playing silly buggers.' And he settled down to the drive, feeling vaguely foolish and slightly fizzy.

After five or six miles, he began to feel really washed-out. Maybe it was an accumulation of travel-weariness and tension: the long trip, together with the hot-rodding of fifteen minutes before; but whatever the reason, Keith felt less than well — desperately tired and uncomfortably dozy. He bore it for another ten minutes or so, until he reached a village on the road. A floodlit pub-sign, the Bird in Hand, was mounted on a tall mast at the verge and Keith swung the wheel over, crunching across the gravel on to the small car-park.

A freshener, he decided; that was what he needed. Not too long, now, before he reached home. A pick-me-up would see him back nicely.

Although there was only half-an-hour or so before closing-time, the pub was nearly empty. Four locals sat at a plain wooden table, playing cribbage; a pair of teenage lovers, as far from anyone else as they could get, mooned over each other, speaking in soft voices and ignoring their drinks; two tall, beefy men who looked like truck drivers were occupying a table by the window and peering out into the dim light provided for the car-park by a single lamp above the pub door. The landlord was sitting at the bar, next to a middle-aged couple. They had a seed catalogue spread out on the bar-towels and were deep in dispute.

With some reluctance, and still talking, the landlord got down from his stool and went round to the other side of the bar. Keith smiled as he got his 'Good evening' and asked for a large brandy, which he took to a table. The first sip revived him. He screwed his fists into his eye-sockets and worked at the tiny muscles there until yellow and red flashes swam up in the darkness, then watched the blurred edges of things come back into focus as he reached out for his glass. A hand was flat on the table next to it. On each finger, between the second and third joints, was tattooed a letter. The letters spelt 'LOVE'. It was a thick, powerful arm that led to the hand, the bicep stretching the rolled-up shirt-sleeve into a taut cord. The second man looked over from the table by the window, his lips pursed round a cigarette in a half-smile.

The man who had come over to Keith's table spoke in a low voice, but a voice thick with aggression and cluttered with brutish vowel-sounds. 'Was that you in the white Datsun back there, squire?'

Keith's stomach went liquid and a small electric shock seemed to zip through his skull. The man jerked his head in the direction of the car-park.

'White Datsun,' he repeated. 'Saw you drive in just now.'

'That's my car, yes.'

'Having a little game, were we? On the road back there?'

'I don't know about that.' Keith made an attempt to sound bluff, as if the incident hadn't impressed him as being of much importance. 'I know that you were driving too close — blinding me, with your headlights full up.'

The man looked over his shoulder to where his friend sat and nodded slowly. Then he turned back. 'I almost came unstuck a couple of times there, mate.' He menaced Keith with a pause, then went on: 'I could have come to grief there.'

Keith knew that the rights and wrongs of the affair, any notion of justice, or the judgment that might be given by some theoretical, independent observer, mattered less than nothing. Even so, he said, 'You started it,' modifying its brusqueness with, 'be fair.' Then reached for his brandy.

117

Before he could grasp the glass, the man extended a finger, stabbing on to the back of Keith's hand and pinning it palm-down to the table. He lifted Keith's glass, drank off the brandy, and then tossed the glass casually into Keith's lap. He continued to stare down for a moment or two, but when his look wasn't met, turned and went to the door. The other got up and followed him out.

After the door closed Keith went over to the window, clutching his brandy glass, turning his back on the curious eyes in the room. A dark-coloured Ford was pulling out on to the road, the word 'Capri' stencilled on the back in a large, glittering, silver-and-red script, luminous where it caught some light from the outside lamp. When Keith ordered a second drink, the landlord served it to him wordlessly, slapping the change down on the bar. Keith nodded his thanks, caught the landlord's eye for a moment and tried for a wry smile, but it wouldn't hold. He walked back to his table where he sipped his drink for a while before the silence became really nervy, at which point he tossed the remains of the liquor back and left.

Five minutes after setting off, he saw a car parked unevenly on the grass verge in the narrow lane, its emergency stop lights flashing. A figure, indistinct, standing on the nearside and away from the road, was waving an arm. Perhaps it was tiredness, perhaps it had to do with an instinct to obey what might have been a warning about some danger ahead; or simply that the scene signalled 'breakdown' – someone stuck on a country road and needing help. In any case, Keith didn't make what, for some, would have been an obvious connection. He slowed almost to a stop, paying more attention to where he should pull on to the grass than to the other car and the waving figure. As he began to wind his window down, he saw the garish transfer on the other car's boot and his heart seemed to miss half-a-dozen beats. Cranking the handle furiously, he struggled to raise the window; then realizing that this was only delaying him, he tried to snap down the lock on his door while, at the same time, fumbling for reverse. He got the lock down, but the gear-lever slipped from his perspiring palm and sprang back into neutral. In the same instant, there came a terrific crash on the roof of the car.

The second man had appeared and was yanking at the doors; then he started to lash at the windows – as the other had done on the roof – with something that flailed from his grip, trailing back, then smashing against the glass.

'Chains,' thought Keith, 'they're using chains.' He was shivering with fear, hardly able to grip the gear-lever. His foot was hard down on the accelerator: terrified in case the engine might stall. The two men walked almost casually round the car, as if looking for vulnerable points, flogging the glass and bodywork with their chains.

Keith found the gear and let the clutch in with an unwieldy thump. The car leapt back, churning grass and gravel, the wheels hissing and skidding, until they found the road surface. The men ran after him, whipping the chains down on the bonnet. Clear of them for a moment, Keith slammed the car into first, revved the engine and drove straight at them. They had anticipated this. As he roared between them, one brought his chain down hard, aiming at the offside window – at Keith's face. The links struck a glancing blow, cracking the glass, then slid away as he accelerated past. Dimly he heard a voice roar something: a curse or a shout of frustration as he escaped. Then he was clear, flooring the pedal as he barrelled down the narrow lane.

He drove like a maniac, sure that they would soon be in pursuit. At each bend, he slammed through the gears, torturing the engine and praying that he wouldn't meet anything coming the other way as he took three-quarters of the road on each curve.

At any minute, he expected to see lights in his rear-view mirror. But there was nothing apart from his own head-

119

lights illuminating hedgerows and fields of wheat; nothing but the sound of his own car: the whinny of tyres as he cornered, the drone and shriek of the overtaxed engine.

He didn't relax until he reached the town. Even then, he drove a long circuit before cruising down his own street. There was no sign of the Capri. He heaved on the wheel and steered across the dip in the pavement where it met the short, concrete strip that led to his carport. A slight *clank-clank* that he had heard as he toured the town was still there: clearly, his attackers had done some damage, though he couldn't pinpoint the noise. He would look in the morning. Right now, he felt ragged with tiredness and sick, as if fear had soured his stomach.

He had to lean on the battered door to get it open. It gave suddenly and he all but fell on to the driveway. The *clank* came again. Keith climbed out, pushed the door back as best he could, and bent down to see what was making the noise. Wound round the door handle, lashed there by the force of the blow, was a bicycle chain, two-thirds of its length trailing down the side of the door. It was looped at the bottom, the links jammed against each other and locked where it had been gripped. Jammed in the loop, its bloody stump a mess of skin-flaps, white tendon and glistening stick of bone, was a human finger. Between the knuckle and the unplugged spike of the finger-bone, still visible on the obscenely rucked skin, was a blue, tattooed letter 'L'.

Words to the Unwise

The sky was a deep, glum grey, promising rain. Beyond the harbour, the sea was flecked with white where the stiff wind toppled the crests of even the smallest waves. Carrie Andrews stood on the quayside holding baby Jonathan so that his face was tucked into her shoulder: turned away from the light spume blowing off the water. Miranda, her five-year-old, clutched at Carrie's skirt. She would have liked to have held Carrie's hand, but that wasn't possible – many things that she liked, things that made her feel secure and special, had become 'not possible' since baby Jonathan had been born. She looked up at her mother, who was arranging the baby's shawl to better protect him from the blow. 'When are we getting on the boat, Mummy?' she asked.

Carrie said, 'Soon. They'll tell us when.' She said it without looking down.

'When will we be in Ireland?'

'Tomorrow.'

'And then we'll see Daddy?'

'That's right.'

'Will he come to meet us?'

'Yes.' Carrie sighed and tucked the shawl tightly round

121

the baby's sleeping face. 'Yes, I'm sure he'll come to meet us.' She pictured him standing by the door of the arrivals hall, impatient, eager to install them in the new house so that he could get back to work. She could almost feel his perfunctory kiss, hear his chivvying voice as he hurried them along. She summoned up these images knowing how they would depress her, but knowing that they were pretty accurate versions of what would happen. She hadn't wanted to go — she still didn't and for a moment toyed with the idea of taking the children back to her parents' house in Marlow and telephoning Stephen from there to say, openly for the first time, what they both knew to be true: that their marriage was a shambles, that there was no real feeling left between them, that she had been happy for the first time for a long time during the two months of their separation.

He had gone to Ireland to advise on an especially difficult project: the building of a new power-plant. His company had promoted him and paid him a sizeable bonus for the 'inconvenience' of having to be apart from his family. Now the job looked like taking much longer than anyone had anticipated; a house had been found and Carrie and the children sent for. 'Inconvenience' was the company's term for the separation. To Carrie it was more like freedom — freedom from the bickering, the fallings-out, the sad, love-less existence she had lived for more than a year. She thought again about going back to Marlow, but knew she wouldn't do it. Arrangements had been made; they were on their way; her sorrow and the reasons for it had as much to do with her lack of independence as anything else, and secretly she knew that.

It was time to board. An attendant showed them to their cabin, fussing over them because they were travelling on their own. He hefted the suitcases on to the lower bunk and accepted the fifty-pence piece that Carrie slipped into his hand.

'Are we in for a rough crossing?' Carrie asked.

'I wouldn't be at all surprised.' He peered out of the porthole. 'The cloud's not lifting. There'll be some rain and a fair blow, I'd guess. You won't be too bad down here. It's those above who'll feel it worst. This,' he unlatched the porthole and swung it open, 'comes undone like that — see, the catch at the side here. If you get to feeling queasy, you can pop your head out perhaps, and get some sea air.'

She thanked him and set about unpacking a few things that they would need for the night. 'Miranda,' she said, 'you can go in the top bunk — you climb up that tiny ladder there. Won't that be exciting?' She tried to lighten her tone, but suddenly felt very close to tears. She was past the point of no return. 'The baby can sleep with me in the bottom bunk.'

Miranda made no effort to keep the tears back. 'Can't I? Can't I sleep with you, Mummy? I'll be frightened.'

'Miranda, behave!' Carrie snapped irritably. At once she tried to soften the annoyance in her voice — 'Jonathan's only a baby; you're a big girl now, aren't you?' But it was too late. The child walked over to a corner of the cabin and stood there facing the wall.

Jonathan woke and started to cry. Carrie laid him on the upper bunk while she shifted the suitcases, then sat down with him in a chair under the porthole to feed him. Miranda peeked. Even though it fascinated her to watch, Jonathan's feeds were what she resented most. The small, downy head placidly at the breast, her mother's gift of her own body to the baby, was an intimacy that excluded her entirely. She felt utterly left out, cut off from Carrie's time and her attention. She peeked and bit her lip in anger. In some obscure way, she connected her father's absence with the baby. He had left only a week or so after the birth. Miranda had wanted to go with him, but that had been another 'not possible'. Her father had gone completely, her mother had withdrawn into a world occupied by herself and Jonathan, emerging only to attend to Miranda's most basic needs. She

123

had found, at first, that she could get Carrie's attention by behaving badly, but that technique worked for a short time only. Very soon, she found her tantrums were distancing her mother even more: she would be shuffled off on to Granny Cooper and taken away from Carrie — to a park, for a walk by the river or to the shops; on these occasions, she could be grumpy and demand sweets or ice-cream as compensation, but she knew she had been outmanoeuvred.

More galling than anything was the fact that everyone agreed that Jonathan was a 'good baby'. He slept often, rarely cried for no reason, was tractable and happy. 'He's a good baby,' visitors would coo, as Jonathan wriggled on a blanket by the hearth. 'You are lucky to have such a good baby.' Although she couldn't rationalize her feelings, Miranda felt in all this praise some criticism of herself, so she was particularly pleased when Jonathan's feed failed to have the usual effect. Instead of burbling happily for a time before going back to sleep, he cried without ceasing for almost an hour.

Carrie paced up and down the small cabin, patting the baby's back and murmuring to comfort him. Her voice was low, but there was tension in it. From time to time, she would stop patting and rake her hand through her hair in a gesture of muted hysteria. They had been at sea for a long time before the baby quietened and eventually fell into a light doze. Carrie lowered him on to the bottom bunk as if she were trying to set down a piece of ash and keep it intact, then she arranged the pillows along the side, to keep him there. She glanced at her watch. The porthole showed a circular cut of darkening sea and sky.

'Miranda, it's time for you to go to sleep as well.'

The girl pouted. 'I'm hungry.'

'You had an enormous tea,' Carrie snapped. 'There's some milk for you in the flask and you can have a biscuit. But it's bedtime.'

'What are you going to do?'

124

'After you're in bed, I'm going to have some supper upstairs.' *And a drink*, she thought. 'You'll be perfectly all right. I won't be far away.'

'Can't I come with you?' The tears were back in Miranda's eyes. 'No, it's not possible, Miranda. Please be good. *Please.*' Carrie turned away and began to unpack the child's night-clothes and the flask of milk. The boat was rolling a good deal and she spilt a gout of milk on to the floor as she tried to pour it.

'Two biscuits,' Miranda said.

'Yes, for God's sake, two biscuits!' Carrie shouted the words and Jonathan woke and began to howl. Carrie breathed in and held the breath for a long time. She let it out in a monotone of curses sewn together. Miranda got into bed with her biscuits and watched her mother pacing to and fro again, teetering with the motion of the boat, having to put a hand out now and then to steady herself. Jonathan sensed the uncertainty and wouldn't be consoled.

Five times Carrie managed to calm the child and five times he woke again mere seconds after she had put him back on the bunk. She paced and patted, becoming more desperate and distraught by the minute; she was hungry and miserable and she badly needed a drink; she said, 'Jonathan, do shut up. For Christ's sake shut up. Go to sleep Jonathan. For God's sake, go to sleep.' His crying was like a fingernail scraping across slate. 'Shut up, Jonathan. Do, please, please, shut up. If you don't shut up, I'll stifle you, Jonathan. If you don't shut up, I'll put you out of the porthole. I'll put you out of the porthole, Jonathan. Do shut up. Please. Please. Please.'

Miranda said, 'Isn't he naughty?' She was delighted; she hadn't even bothered to use Carrie's distress − the likelihood that she would take the easy way out − to get bribes of more biscuits and milk. The baby's yelling dimmed to a series of whimpers. Carrie continued to pace with him, scarcely daring to angle her head to see whether he was starting to doze. When his whimpering faded too, she counted to three hundred, before risking a look. He was asleep. Trying to ride with the boat's movement, she got to the bunk and put him down, gentling his head until the very last. She straightened up and looked at Miranda, placing a finger on her lips, then pulled the blankets up as the girl settled to sleep. 'I won't be long,' she whispered.

The first gin and tonic was the best, but the second tasted pretty good too. She had been too late for dinner, though she had long since passed the stage where she much cared. Between drinks, she had gone back to the cabin, tiptoeing up to the door to listen without going in. There had been no sound. She was a little ashamed of herself for having been so angry with Jonathan — and with Miranda. She knew how the girl felt, and she knew why. The child probably *had* been treated unfairly; a new baby shouldn't be a source of resentment. Carrie resolved to try harder with Miranda: to show her more affection and give her more attention. Nothing, though, could make her resolve to try harder with Stephen. The more she brooded on their unhappiness, the more determined she became to sort the matter out — for better, she thought wryly, or worse. She sealed the determination with a last drink, then went back to the cabin, swaying along the narrow corridors, feeling pleasantly drowsy and just a little tipsy.

The attendant who had carried her suitcase heard the scream: heard it over the rumble of engine, heard its rawness and fright. When he entered the cabin, Carrie was standing close to the open porthole, her eyes wide, her nails scoring red lines down her cheeks. Miranda was sitting up in bed, crying, wearing an expression of distressed, confused innocence. She turned to the attendant for support. 'I only did what Mummy said,' she wailed. He looked at her, uncomprehendingly. 'He woke up and cried and wouldn't shut up. I only did what Mummy said.'

The Revenge

He was sure — quite sure. Previously, there had been nothing more than suspicion, but now Bert Rawlinson was quite sure that his wife was being unfaithful to him. The signs had been there for three or four weeks — maybe longer, he reasoned, since he wasn't likely to have been alert to them at the beginning. The first thing he had noticed was that her tendency to have a headache at bedtime had increased, though her unaccustomed jollity each morning, as she pecked his cheek by the front door, didn't seem entirely in keeping with the drubbing migraine that had pole-axed her the night before. Then there had been the silent phone calls; he would lift the receiver and recite the number, only to hear a click followed by the impenetrable purr of the dialling tone. They were part of a pattern that included Barbara's cryptic calls. If the telephone rang at about eight o'clock in the evening, she would make a little too much of an effort to be the one to answer it. 'I'll get it,' she would call, or, 'That's probably for me.' There would then follow a series of one-word answers that gave no indication of what was being said by the caller. 'Yes, no, O.K., fine, no, no, yes, all right, goodbye,' would be something akin to a typical response. Afterwards, she would claim that it had been her mother, arranging to meet her in town for a coffee the following morning, or a girlfriend suggesting they go to the cinema together. Or a friend from her evening-class.

The evening-class — there was something a bit peculiar about that, too. Barbara had never until then shown the slightest inclination to take her education any further than the point at which she had left it when she was sixteen; then, just a few weeks before, she announced that she had signed up for a French course. Classes took place, it seemed, every Tuesday from seven o'clock until nine. Quite soon, she had taken to joining a regular trip to the pub after the class, with 'a few of the other girls on the course', so she was rarely home before ten-thirty on those nights. She would have known that Bert wouldn't have wanted to join the class too; and, in any case, he never arrived back on Tuesdays before seven-thirty. Bert earned his living by driving short-haul trips for a company that sold ready-mixed concrete. The more trips he made, the more he earned. On Tuesdays (and he knew that Barbara knew this) there were always late deliveries and the chance to make some overtime. They needed the money badly, so he always drove the extra trips. His practice, now, was to fry himself some eggs and watch television until Barbara returned. Once or twice — especially lately, since he was testing her more as his suspicion grew — he had suggested that he join them in the pub. Barbara told him — firmly, but with what seemed like a touch of panic in her voice — that no, that wasn't a good idea, they didn't always go to the same pub, he wouldn't like the other girls much, he would be bored, and, anyway, it was a break for her to get out now and then and talk girl-talk with friends; until he said O.K., O.K., she was probably right, he would be bored.

Once the thought that she was cheating on him was in his mind, he began to detect the sinister in almost everything she said or did. And, ironically, it was his own recognition of the fact that his mind was loaded with dark thoughts that provided him with proof of Barbara's infidelity. Could it be, he reasoned during one of his agonized weighings of hint and uncertainty, could it be that the whole thing was a figment of his obsessed imagination? He reasoned that it could. He also reasoned that to confess his unfair, unkind suspicions wouldn't be likely to soothe those night-time headaches. It would also (the balance swung back again, from probable innocence to possible guilt) alert her and put her on her guard if she *were* having an affair.

His means of discovering the truth wasn't particularly subtle; it was forthright and effective. He telephoned the College of Further Education where Barbara claimed to be taking her French lessons. He had devised a rather clumsy excuse for having her called to the phone: a delivery man would have arrived at the door, claiming that a new vacuum cleaner had been ordered; Bert would be checking to make sure that the man was mistaken — and, of course, it would be clear that he had got the wrong address. Barbara would be cross, of course; but Bert would be reassured. He had made the call. They had never heard of Barbara Rawlinson. Yes, they were sure. Yes, there was a French course given on Tuesday evenings. Yes, he had got the right College. No, there was definitely no one of that name taking the course.

When Barbara got back that evening, she found him engrossed in a TV thriller. He barely looked up as she came into the room, though a little later, just before she took her three-tablet dose of aspirin, he bothered to ask her how the lesson had gone.

'Fine,' she said.

'And did you have a good gossip at the pub?'

'It was O.K.; they're not a bad bunch. I think I might have had one too many, though. My head's splitting.'

'Who are they?'

'What? Who are who?'

He turned to face her. 'The girls.'

'I told you. People from the class.'

'Yes, love, I know; I mean, what are their names?'

'That's an odd thing to ask.' She looked shifty. 'Why should you want to know that? Did you remember to ask your father if you could borrow the car on Sunday? He did get the tyre changed, I suppose?' She was speaking quickly, trying to turn him and he knew it. 'Was it the tyre,' she persisted, 'or something else?'

He turned back to the TV. 'It was the tyre,' he said. 'Yes, he got it changed.' A moment later, he heard the bedroom door close.

For a couple of days, Bert kept his peace, trying not to let his wife see any change in him while he decided what his next move should be. He felt hurt and miserable, he felt angry, he felt confused, but mostly he felt very foolish; and he wanted his revenge on the man who was making him feel that way before he threw Barbara out of the house. He was looking forward to that: to the moment when he would catch them together. For that, eventually, was what he made his mind up to do.

Each morning for the next three days, he left the house as if to go to work, walking to the nearby bus-stop and getting on the bus when it came along. Instead of completing the trip, though, he would go only as far as the town, where he would have a cup of coffee before catching a bus back to within one stop of his own street. Leaving the pavements of the small estate, he would then approach his house through a small meadow, taking care to skirt the place so that Barbara wouldn't catch sight of him if she happened to be looking through the kitchen window.

He never saw the man arrive or leave, since he could watch only the back of the house; but he saw him well enough – in the lounge, drinking coffee, in the kitchen with his arms wrapped around Barbara's waist as she rinsed the cups at the sink, in the bedroom, in *his* bedroom, standing behind Barbara as she twitched the curtains together. Through the narrow gap between his own house and his neighbour's, Bert could see an open-topped sports car parked, cunningly enough, across the boundary where the gardens joined so that you couldn't have been quite sure who the driver might have been visiting. On each of the three days of Bert's sad vigil, it was there; on each day, the man was there; on the third day, Bert caught a glimpse of him removing his shirt as the curtains closed.

That weekend, they made their monthly trip to Barbara's parents in the borrowed car. Bert was quiet, but made an attempt to seem affable. Once or twice, he sensed that Barbara was watching him curiously and he felt a touch of panic at the notion that she might warn her boyfriend off: he was living for Monday morning, for the confrontation. He had something special planned and the anticipation of it was the only thing that kept him from taking his wife by the throat. With some effort, he lightened his mood, joining in the chatter until Barbara and her mother retired to the kitchen, leaving the men to the Sunday papers. Bert looked at the newsprint, reading the words, but didn't take them in; camouflaged behind the *Sunday Express,* he gloated through his gloom.

Next morning, he went to work in the usual way and reported to the office.

'Feeling better?' his boss asked him.

'I don't know what it was: some bug or another. Yes, I'm fine now.'

He made a couple of trips, getting back for the third load at about ten o'clock. On the third trip, however, he took a different route, swinging off the trunk road and taking the tipper truck through the town and parking it a half-mile or so from his house. He crossed the meadow and watched. The car was parked in its accustomed place; Barbara's boyfriend was sipping coffee in the lounge.

Bert waited until they reached the bedroom before re-tracing his steps to the truck. His street was empty when he reached it, but it would have made little difference if there had been people about – Bert wasn't going to be stopped now. He coasted down towards his house, keeping the engine noise to a minimum, then pulled across the road and reversed up to the open-topped car. He really didn't have to use the wing-mirrors; the technique was second nature by this time. There was a soft rumble, like a distant landslide, and the sluice at the back of the truck filled with concrete. The glutinous, grey mass slopped into the car, over the upholstery, over the carpets, spreading and piling, until the floor was covered, then the base of the seats. Still Bert kept jacking the drum up, directing the load accurately. The door-handles disappeared, then the lower half of the steering-wheel, until the car filled completely and concrete began to spill over the sides and slither down into the road.

Bert reversed the drum, pulling away from the car so that he could lean out and look back. He smiled. Then he put the truck into gear and drove it into the next street before walking slowly back to where the car stood, brimming with hardening concrete. There was a lamp-post a few yards along the street on the opposite side; he walked over and leaned against it, lighting a cigarette and waiting for the front door of his house to open.

Four cigarettes later, he saw the outline of Barbara's head puddling dimly on the frosted glass of the door. A second outline swam against hers for a moment as the man kissed her, then the door opened and he walked down the path towards the gate while Barbara stood in the doorway to see him off. He paused at the gate and looked back, blowing her a kiss, getting one in return. Neither of them saw Bert. The man came out of the gateway, turning left, away from the ruined car. He walked ten or fifteen feet to the lamp-post directly opposite to Bert's. He was whistling a tune from

Oklahoma! Secured to the lamp-post by a heavy chain was an expensive racing bicycle. Barbara's lover stopped to peg his trouser-bottoms with bicycle clips, unfastened the chain and lobbed it into the saddle bag, then threw a leg over the bike and set off down the road. Bert stood and watched him go, unable to move. He could hear the man's fluting whistle for some time after he had turned the corner into the next street.

Going Home

'Five hundred thousand lire?' Marco Buonorotti stared at the railway official in unaffected horror.

'Si.' The official met Marco's pop-eyed stare, then shrugged, at the same time lifting his left hand, palm upwards, in a gesture that said *Tough luck; I don't fix the charges; take it or leave it.*

'Five hundred thousand lire!' Marco slapped the table (disgust), then slapped his forehead (despair), then slapped his bicep, crooking his arm at the same time (unmistakable gesture needing no interpretation), and left the small office. His father and brother were sitting patiently on a bench in the middle of the station waiting-area. They were wearing black, as Marco was wearing black, and their faces were solemn, befitting men in deep mourning.

'It's five hundred thousand lire,' said Marco and sat down on the bench.

With one accord his father and brother rose; it was as if an electric shock had been passed through the rusty metal slats. They stood over him, looking as he had looked when the railway clerk had given him the news; then his younger brother, Dino, grinned and slapped him on the shoulder. 'You're kidding us, aren't you?'

134

A harder slap canted Dino's head sideways. 'Idiot!' snapped his father. 'Marco wouldn't make jokes about this − with your grandfather not yet in his coffin.' The anger went as quickly as it had come. 'It would not be fitting,' he added, to mollify the young man, 'you'll learn as you grow older.' He turned his attention to Marco. 'Five hundred thousand?' Marco nodded. His father turned away, hissing between his teeth. Marco got up and went to him, putting an arm round the slumped shoulders.

'Well, Papa; we cannot do it.'

'We must . . . somehow.' There was fire in the older man's eyes. 'He will be buried in the south, in Sicily. We'll take him back to Agrigento, the place where he was born. It is a matter of honour.'

That evening, after the meal had been eaten, the three men sat round their table drinking wine and trying to find a solution. The women − Marco's mother, his grandmother and his wife − sat silently by, sewing. When they had been given the news, they had done their fair share of wailing, of flapping their hands and wishing all manner of ill on the railway, its officials, its rolling stock and its price tariffs. Now they sat by, quietly, as the men talked the problem over.

Roberto Buonorotti's father had lived a long life. He had died only twelve hours before, at an age that could only be guessed at; Roberto thought he was a hundred or there-abouts: no one knew for sure. The family had lived in Bergamo, in the north of Italy, for many years. Roberto had been taken there as a child by his parents, who had expected to find work there, and wealth. They had travelled back to Sicily only three times, but on each occasion, Roberto's father had told him: 'This is where you shall bring me when I die. To bury me here, where my roots are. The south.' Now it was time for the old man to make his last journey south . . . it was time, but it was impossible. The railway's price for transporting body and coffin, for going to

the trouble of organizing its safe and secure passage, for
tackling the forms and procedures that officialdom re-
quires, was five hundred thousand lire. That, together with
the fares for the live members of the family and the cost of
the funeral itself, would add up to a sum of money that the
Buonorottis simply didn't possess.

The men drank and smoked and dismissed each other's
suggestions and grew increasingly gloomy. Borrowing the
money was out of the question: for one thing, they would
have a hard time paying it back; for another, they didn't
know anyone who could lend it to them. The notion of
speeding along major highways with the coffin strapped to
the roof rack offended their sense of dignity; but even if it
hadn't, the idea was impossible, since they didn't possess a
car and none of them could drive. As the empty wine
bottles disappeared from the table and were replaced with
full ones, their anger grew.

'Five hundred thousand lire!' Marco spat. 'Have they no
respect for the dead? A living man travels for sixty thous-
and. A dead man must be charged five hundred thou. . . '
He broke off and looked at his father. 'A living man travels
for sixty thousand,' he repeated, keeping his voice low so
that the women wouldn't hear.

'Impossible.' Roberto looked at his son in amazement but
matched his whisper. 'Think of your grandmother, your
mother. Could they sit there beside him and not show grief?
Think of the indignity. And what of the other passengers?'
he asked.

'He will seem to be sleeping — there's nothing odd about
that. They will see an old man who has fallen asleep.'

Marco pondered the other question and glanced over to
where the women sat. 'And they must go first to arrange
things, see the priest, make sure that everything is in order.'

'And what will we tell them?' Roberto asked.

'To trust us: that we will find a way. We'll worry about
what they should be told when the funeral is over.'

Dino joined in the whispering. 'You really think that we can get away with it — taking him on the train with us as a passenger?'

Marco nodded. 'To the station in a taxi; to the train in his wheelchair; then he . . . sleeps . . . until we reach Agrigento.'

'And what happens when we have to change trains?'

'The wheelchair again.'

The three men looked at one another. Roberto poured more wine, then walked over to the women. 'Tomorrow you must travel to Agrigento and wait for us there. We will find a way to take Papa home. Trust us; we will find a way.'

The taxi-driver had to be bribed, but that was the only hitch. Once they arrived at the busy station in the twilight of mid-evening two days later, no one paid them any attention. The old man was swathed in a large travelling-rug and appeared to be fast asleep. Whenever possible, Roberto and his sons stood in front of the chair, blocking the corpse from view. The two younger men flanked it, now, as they moved quickly along the platform looking for an empty carriage as far from the ticket barrier as possible.

Roberto was still smarting from the taxi-driver's insulting laughter. They had had to tell him everything, believing that since he was known to them, he would sympathize. He had taken their money, laughing uproariously. He had laughed all the way to the station. Each of the men had secretly vowed that the cackling fool would be dealt with when they returned.

While Marco held his dead grandfather in his arms, Dino folded the wheelchair. Then they boarded the train and entered the compartment they had selected. Dino took the chair back along the train and stowed it in the guard's van, while the other two settled the old man into a corner seat, covering him with the rug, making sure he was firmly wedged-in, and finally sitting one either side of him. When

137

Dino returned, he paused a moment outside and looked in. The scene looked entirely convincing; his grandfather really did seem to be sleeping: slumped a little to one side, eyes firmly closed, the rumpled rug disguising the fact that his chest wasn't rising and falling. In any case, reasoned Dino, who would look for that — or pay them any attention? To be on the safe side, though, their plan was to spread themselves around the compartment and try to discourage others from coming in.

The train was only twenty minutes late pulling out of the station. As it began to move, Roberto looked at his sons and smiled. 'We are taking him home,' he said. 'I promised; and we have found a way.' There were tears in his eyes. Marco reached into the cardboard suitcase that held their belongings, and produced a bottle of *grappa*. He uncapped it and passed it to his father, who swigged, wiped the neck of the bottle and handed it on to Dino. They had each taken four drinks before Roberto turned to look out of the window, at the roofscape fading in the dwindling light. 'We are taking you home, Papa,' he said, one hand patting the thick folds of the rug; with the other he reached out for the bottle again.

After an hour or so, they were all drunk and comfortably maudlin. The bottle was empty, their hearts were full, tears flowed with intermittent vigour and anecdotes about the old man's bravery and honour, his hard life nobly borne, were embellished with unabashed extravagance. At some point it was decided that a series of toasts should be drunk to Roberto's father: to his courage, to his unblemished character, to his devoutness and to the certainty that he would prosper in the hereafter. But the bottle was undeniably empty.

Roberto rose. 'We will drink the toasts', he declared, 'at the bar. It is in the next coach.'

'Leave him?' asked Dino. 'We can't just leave him.'

Marco nodded. 'No one has come in; no one will. He's just an old man, sleeping. What could happen?' He got up

138

and joined his father at the door of the compartment where
the pair of them swayed, very unsteadily, with the motion
of the train. 'We will drink the toasts and be back very
soon.' His voice was thick with the *grappa*, but a fierceness
was in him, communicated by his father. 'Come on,' he
took his brother by the shoulder. 'Come and drink to his
memory.'

On all long train journeys, there are those who will settle
in, establish themselves in a carriage, then, finally, find
their way to the bar; there are others who will first find their
way to the bar, and worry about inessentials later. Some
people, of course, don't visit the bar at all: people who take
with them bottles of soft drink and mineral water. The ways
of such people are unknowable to the devout; they live in a
strange world of order and sobriety and wake each morning
to bright-eyed clarity; they know nothing of the terror of
recollection gradually restored.

As the Buonorotti men shouldered their way through the
late-night drinkers, they passed a table at which sat four
people, two men and two girls. Their suitcases were stacked
around a table that bristled with bottles. They had been
drinking, the foursome, since the train had pulled out: not
fervently, perhaps, but with increasing dedication. Now
the girls were tired, so the taller of the two men went to the
bar for a double round, the last of the evening. He returned
with the drinks, squeezing past the Buonorottis who were
inventing ingenious toasts, and smiled at his girl who was
dozing with a glass in her hand.

'O.K., Paolo,' he said to the other man. 'Bedtime.'

They downed their drinks and nudged the girls who
downed half of theirs, then all four left the bar to the
drinkers of toasts and the keepers of vigils and went in
search of seats.

'. . . Just an old man, sleeping,' Paolo was saying. 'It's the
best there is.' The others peered in through the glass. They

139

had wanted to be on their own – none was quite *that* drunk – but they had searched in vain for an empty compartment. Reluctantly, they slid the door back and ranged themselves along the seat facing the sleeper, the girls giggling at his sombre expression. Paolo waggled a hand before the old man's face, playing to the gallery, then swung the final suitcase up on to the rack and fell back into the seat opposite.

The four went to sleep almost immediately, lulled by the drink and the gentle rocking of the train. Ten minutes later, they all came awake simultaneously. The train had slowed harshly for some reason. In the bar, drinks were spilled and people lost their footing on the wet floor. Roberto Buonorotti cursed as his glass cracked against his teeth and *grappa* flowed down his shirt-front. In the carriage, Paolo's girl slipped from the crook of his elbow and cannoned into her friend; the taller man, who had propped his frame across the width of the carriage, crashed between the two seats, smacking his shoulder-blades on the floor; the suitcase above the old man's head slid off the rack before Paolo could straighten up to catch it and descended on to the lolling head with a terrible crack. The old man pitched sideways and lay motionless along the length of the seat. Paolo's girl screamed faintly: a sound that mingled with the squeal of the brakes as the train came to a complete halt.

'He can't be dead!' Paolo looked at his friend in horror. The taller man let go of the cadaver's wrist; the arm fell like a lopped branch. 'He is. That blow from the suitcase must have done for him.' In the stopped train, surrounded by a country silence, their whispers seemed like shouts.

'We must call the guard,' one of the girls said. 'We'll have to report it to someone.'

'And they take our names and addresses,' Paolo observed, 'and we have to appear in court and testify to what happened, and your parents find out where you both really were – and who you were really with!'

The girl put a hand over her mouth. 'What else can we do?' she asked, biting at her fingers. The men looked at one another. Then the taller of the two went out into the corridor, holding the compartment door open.

'No one,' he whispered. There was a door immediately opposite the compartment. 'No one!'

One at the head, one at the feet, the rug still covering his torso and legs; it wasn't a difficult task. The old man was a lightweight and they were able to throw him quite a way once they had descended on to the track: well out of range of the lights from the carriage windows.

'His case, too. That brown suitcase!'

Paolo stood on the track as the Buonorottis' shabby cardboard suitcase was handed down to him. Then he walked a couple of paces and hurled it after the dead man, before clambering back and returning to the compartment. The four looked at each other, breathing heavily. One of the girls lit a cigarette and started to say something: 'Do you think . . . ' She paused as the train was tugged, tugged again, then started to glide forwards, gathering speed, the wheels producing a rhythmic double tick that grew increasingly rapid. 'Do you think . . . ' she repeated; but couldn't finish the sentence.

Dino chuckled as he sponged his father's shirt-front. 'I think enough drunks have been toasted.' The garbled advice made Marco splutter into his drink.

'You are right,' agreed Roberto. 'We must – ' He waved a hand in the general direction of their carriage. Marco licked the dregs from his glass. 'We must,' he echoed and led the way down the corridor, bracing himself on either side with outstretched arms.

All three glanced into their carriage, saw the two men and two women, and walked straight past. They had almost reached the front of the train before they realized that something was wrong. More puzzled than alarmed, they retraced their steps to the bar. Then, more alarmed than puzzled, went back at twice the pace, scrutinizing each compartment as if searching for someone they would only half-recognize. Dino stopped by a door and waited for the others to catch up.

'I'm sure it was here: that torn blind, the numbers of the seats . . .'

The four people in the compartment sat still, not sleeping, not lounging, having the appearance, rather, of patients in a dentist's waiting-room. Roberto pushed past his son and went in.

'Excuse me.' The men and women looked up. 'We are searching for . . .' Roberto spread his hands and smiled apologetically. What he was about to say would sound preposterous. 'We are looking for an old man; my father. He was asleep. He was wrapped in a rug. We thought . . . this compartment. We thought he was in here when we left.'

It did sound preposterous: but more so, Roberto imagined, to himself and his sons. *They* knew they had lost a corpse; these other people would imagine that a mistake had been made, or that the lost person had wandered off to another part of the train.

One of the young women seemed to be trembling. She had grown very pale and was fumbling in her handbag, searching for a cigarette, then, when she had found it, delving back, frenziedly, for her lighter. Roberto thought she might be afraid, suspecting a ploy for robbery perhaps, so he stepped back towards the door to reassure her.

'You haven't . . . you didn't see him when you came in?' The taller man shook his head. 'He wasn't in this compartment?' continued Roberto, feeling stupid and panicked and afraid.

'The compartment was empty,' Paolo told him. 'Sorry.' He shrugged and smiled.

Five times, Roberto and his sons walked the entire length

of the train, pressing their faces to the glass windows of each compartment, searching the bar and the restaurant, peering into all the lavatories, rummaging among the packing cases and other paraphernalia in the guard's van. The wheelchair was where Dino had left it, wedged between the side of the van and some slatted boxes packed with chickens that stirred and fluttered now and then before sinking, again, into the somnolence of defeat. The three men gathered around the wheelchair, staring at it as though it possessed some sort of oracular power.

'It's impossible,' said Roberto.

'Yes, impossible.' Marco touched the rubber grip fixed to the handle of the chair. 'What can have . . . what can we tell . . . '

Roberto shook his head, slowly, from side to side — a gesture that began as an expression of confusion and hopelessness, extended to become a denial of the undeniable and finally took on the autistic impetus of a metronome. The train clattered on southwards, through the darkness.

The Cop-out

He woke up with his own yell of fright hanging in the room, knowing he had yelled and woken at the sound. There was a needling pain low down in his back. He bore it for a while, staring at the painting on the wall opposite until it arranged itself into the lines and shapes and colours of a field of corn under a hard blue sky. There was a *bastide* in the middle distance; figures in straw hats were bending to reap and gather, and a wagon, drawn by a big, muscular horse, was coming along the wide furrow by the hedge to collect the stooks. He stayed still for two full minutes, looking at the calm scene, then reached back and massaged the place where the arm of the chair had caught him. Finally, he sighed, swung his feet off the stool, and limped over to turn off the hissing blizzard on the TV screen.

The plane had crashed. The inside of the plane had resembled the long, narrow entrance hall to his mother's house. He had been sitting on the heavy rectangular oak chest with the carved lid that had been alongside the staircase ever since he could remember. Through the clear panes of glass above the front door, he had been able to see clumps of cloud and between them the crude embroidery of dun and green fields thirty-two thousand feet below. An air hostess had come out of the kitchen door, followed by his mother. For a moment, he had thought his mother was about to answer a knock at the door and he had struggled to tell her that she mustn't open it; the plane would decompress and they would all be drawn out into the thin mist in a flailing whoosh. Instead, the air hostess had handed him a cup of hot chocolate. His mother was carrying a spoon to scoop the coagulation of skin from its surface.

He had taken the chocolate and seen that it was slopping to and fro in the beaker. The air hostess had seen it too. 'Oh dear,' she said, 'we're tilting.' He had begun to cry as the clouds whipped past the front-door window and the fields spread and grew and separated. His mother had smoothed his hair, clucking reassuringly. 'It's all for the best, Charles,' she told him. His father had come out of the study, laughing cruelly. 'You shouldn't have come, my boy,' he said, then went back into the sanctum where he would be safe.

When the plane hit the ground it had melted and left him standing in the middle of a cornfield. A horse-drawn wagon was collecting the stooks left by the reapers. He had been lost and had known that no one could see him because he was dead.

He poured himself a large whisky and soda, squatted and rose several times to unlatch the pain in his back, then went over to the painting to see where he had been standing. If the plane had come down there, he thought, the wreckage would be in southern France. Was that on the London-Rome route? He'd have to check.

Worries we live with, as we live with hay fever, leaky taps, convolvulus, bad skin, commuter trains . . . Most people feel real fear but rarely. Some events frighten us more than others: a visit to the dentist, childbirth, the sight of someone we love unwell, a street-fight, a plane ride . . . There are, though, people whose fears restrict them, clutching at the heart, stalling their lives.

They can't go out of doors; or they can't be in open,

deserted places. Sometimes it has to do with spiders or tall buildings; sometimes it's just other people. Charles Black wasn't just a nervous flier. The fear was such that he had only to imagine himself on a plane and a mortal dread overtook him. The spiders advanced. The door slammed behind him and locked, leaving him out in the street. It was as acute as any phobia could be. The problem, the reason for his dream, what caused the sleeplessness that had left him ragged with fatigue and catnapping on an armchair, was the sure knowledge that he would have to fly from London to Rome on the morning of the Wednesday of the week after next.

Charles had flown once before, though it wasn't then that he discovered his fear. The fear had always been there, but since he had never imagined that a situation would occur where he would have no choice but to fly, it hadn't afflicted him too much. Sure, he knew he would miss out on a few things. Holidays abroad would be a bit problematical, but if he could persuade a friend to ferry-and-drive to Europe, he wouldn't have to spend a lifetime without getting outside Great Britain. In fact, that was just what he had done on several occasions and had had a great time, too. O.K., he would be unlikely ever to go to America or Africa or Egypt. He would almost certainly never get to Australia. He didn't mind too much. In fact, he hardly ever thought of those restrictions as a problem. There had, after all, been enough problems of a less theoretical sort over the past five years or so. A broken marriage, his mother's death, his father's bitter withdrawal, the way the house had been allowed to go to pot . . .

Then, inauspiciously and at no precisely discernible moment, life had got better; much better. Lots of little improvements, things rationalized, things accomplished. Looking back, he thought it might have begun with his promotion. The disarray and disappointment in his private life had driven him to a fierce concentration on his job. He had always been pretty good at it: not outstanding, but never in trouble. The difference between 'competent' and 'impressive' often has to do with dedication and Charles discovered a dedication born of mild, unresolvable unhappiness. The job's problems were not problems that hurt; they were problems he could tackle. The promotion was inevitable, financially rewarding (which solved a couple of his personal difficulties immediately) and surprised him with a feeling of self-respect he hadn't known for a very long time.

It also meant, now, that he had to fly to Rome on business. He had been in Spain when his mother died, holidaying with a new girlfriend. He hadn't bothered to tell her about his fear − or, rather, had deliberately omitted to; the very intensity of the phobia made him ashamed. The shock of receiving the telegram, its curt 'Mother dead. Funeral Friday', had distracted him to the extent that he had gone along with the girl's efficient organization of a flight from Alicante to Gatwick. It wasn't until they were actually aboard the plane that he started to come apart. What had followed effectively put an end to the relationship. Even now, the recollection of his own behaviour during the two-and-a-half-hour flight caused him to groan out loud and shake his head as if to dislodge the memory. He was well aware of the fact that he couldn't fly again. It wasn't something he could steel himself to, or get through somehow, or endure if he were drunk or sedated. He couldn't fly again: it was as simple and unchangeable as that. Given the immutable part of the problem, he had to find a way of altering other circumstances. He could resign, but didn't want to. He could fake illness, but that would work only on one occasion. He could tell the truth.

Telling the truth is a cinch, except when it is necessary to make a conscious decision to do so; that usually means that there is an option to lie and that the lie is going to be less painful. Charles knew that he could save himself pain by

147

lying once, maybe twice. Finally, though, he would have
to be truthful; he was courageous enough and sensible
enough to see that it might as well be now. Having made
the decision, he went to bed and slept soundly for the first
time in seventy-two hours.

He woke at seven-thirty the next morning and rose immediately. He bathed, shaved, dressed and then, with his
first cup of coffee beside him, telephoned his managing
director. The receiver was lifted on the second ring.

'John, it's Charles Black.'

'Charles. 'Morning.' John Kirkpatrick wasn't surprised
to be telephoned at eight o'clock on a Sunday morning.
Business before anything might well have been his motto,
and if something pressing claimed his attention before the
Sunday papers or the garden he never felt cheated or put
out.

'Look, I wonder if I could drive over. Maybe take you for a
beer before lunch. There's something I want to talk over.'

'Sure. O.K. There's a pub near the Green, the Three
Pigeons; do you know it?' Kirkpatrick lived in a Home
Counties village about forty minutes drive from London – a
place with two discrete communities; Sunday morning at
the pub was a time when the new, well-heeled community
of city commuters mingled with the locals. The locals
mingled right back, seeming not to feel patronized by the
newcomers' *bonhomie* and their pretence of knowing about
cattle and crops.

'Yes, I do. Meet you there about twelve-fifteen?'

'Fine. See you then, Charles.'

He got to the place at a minute or so past twelve and sat in
the car, on the far side of the Green, until he saw his boss
enter the pub. During the drive down, he hadn't permitted
himself to think about what he had to say, knowing that to
dwell on the confrontation might cause him to lose his
nerve. And now, as he ducked beneath the low lintel and
walked towards Kirkpatrick, he still felt resolved and sur-

prisingly calm. After they'd got their drinks and had re-treated to a table by the window overlooking the Green, he came straight to the point.

'I can't go to Rome. At least, not by plane. I can't fly. It's a fear I simply can't overcome; not nervousness, real terror. I've been trying to think of how to tell you — what to do — and it seemed easiest to, well, spill the beans. I *am* sorry, John. I feel a fool, but it makes no difference. I know perfectly well that I'll never get on that plane. I should have said all this earlier: I mean, when you told me about the trip. Maybe I had some notion of getting over it. But not so. I haven't slept . . . it's just not something I can control. Well,' he finished rather lamely, lifting his drink and taking a long pull at it, 'it must seem nutty to you; it's very real to me.'

Kirkpatrick looked out of the window, watching a little party of drinkers occupying a bench between two half-barrels crowded with daffodils. Despite a chilly breeze, they were determined to take every advantage from weekending in clean air. Eventually he took a sip from his pint pot and looked over at Charles.

'How about going by train?' he asked.

Charles said nothing for a full five seconds. Then he found his voice. 'You're serious? I mean, you don't . . . '

'It means you're out of the office for longer than I'd like. Obviously, I'd sooner you went by plane. Just as obviously, you can't. You're the right person to set this deal up; I certainly don't want to lose you . . . or the deal, for that matter. You can't really have been worried about losing your job, or anything like that. Were you?'

'Well, I . . . yes, in point of fact, I was.'

'No, look —' Kirkpatrick swivelled slightly in his chair and faced Charles fully. 'I'm a practical business man. If all the flights to Rome had been suspended for a week, I'd still have sent you, wouldn't I? Of course. I don't mind flying at all; rather enjoy it, actually, so it's difficult for me to under-stand how you must feel about it. But I *do* understand about

149

The Bite and other Apocryphal Tales

being frightened of things: irrationally frightened. Go by train. Simple.'

'John, I'm so grateful. I . . . ' Charles slumped a little in his chair as the tension left him. Then he gave a little laugh. 'Really, I don't quite know what to say. It's very kind of you.' He raised a hand, palm up, in a gesture that underlined his relief and surprise.

'Don't say anything, old boy. You could buy me a drink, though.' Charles went to the bar and ordered them more beer. He felt light-hearted and very happy.

He worked cheerily and efficiently through the next week, able – for the first time since the announcement of the trip – to concentrate properly. His secretary organized the tickets and co-ordinated train-times. Everything proceeded sweetly and according to plan.

He spent the next weekend with his father – partly a charitable act, but partly a way of saying thank you to the fates, or whatever power had organized events in his favour. The old man was as irritating and demanding as ever, but Charles remained pleasantly unruffled, even when he was sneered at for his fear of flying. He cleaned the house up a little, cooked a roast for Sunday luncheon and finally tucked the old boy up with a brandy before making the hour-long drive back to London. Then, next morning, he caught the train to Paris. From there, he would go directly to Rome. He was particularly taken by the fact that he had a *wagon-lit* for the night-journey through France; he had never travelled in one before and it seemed a romantic idea – night attendants bringing coffee and liqueurs, sipping one's drink before falling asleep in the swaying bunk-bed with the dark, French countryside streaming past; then pulling the shutter down and looking forward to waking in the bustle and heat of Rome's central station.

In fact, he was asleep when the plane crashed into the train, and died without waking. The 727 had developed mechanical trouble too far from its take-off point to turn back and too far from its destination to stand a chance of limping in. The newspapers called it the worst accident of the century: not so, of course, but it made a good headline; and the odd combination of plane and train meant that it stayed a focus of attention for longer than the average air or rail disaster might. The tabloids were still squeezing a few column inches from it two days later when John Kirkpatrick boarded the plane that Charles Black would have taken to get to Rome: business, like life, had to go on. The flight was smooth and uneventful.

The Move

When people leave a house they have lived in for a long time — a house where they have been happy — echoes of that happiness float in the empty rooms. Over the stripped floors, between the cobwebs and little pockets of dust, circling by the uncurtained windows: tiny, plangent accumulations of kindness, of soft words, of love freely given, of Christmas and birthday celebrations, the leaving for holidays and the return, of forgiveness and desire, generosity and shared excitements. Not all houses are like that, of course. In some, the brittle signals of hostility and misery, of love squandered and passion abandoned, are everywhere. It was sure, though, that when the Morrisons walked out of the front door of 25 Wordsworth Drive for the last time — as they would next morning — they would leave behind them almost nothing but good feelings: contentment, happy times, memories of the children's laughter dancing like dust motes in the stale air. Just one anxiety seemed likely to disturb the house's sunny atmosphere: a member of the family had gone missing.

They had been packing the last few personal items, leaving out only washing things and the clothes they would put on in the morning, when one of the twins, Jemima, had noticed the absence. She mentioned it to her brother, James. James looked startled and went upstairs to tell his father.

'We can't find Titch anywhere,' he said. There was a tension in him, looking for reassurance.

'I thought she was shut up in your playroom.' George Morrison knelt on a suitcase and snapped the lock into place. 'Have you looked in the cupboards, that sort of thing?'

'Jemima says she's looked everywhere. The door was open.'

'Well, how on earth did that happen?'

'And the dining-room window's open at the top.'

'Ah.'

Sarah Morrison came into the bedroom and saw her husband and her son facing each other speechlessly. 'George?' She looked at him and waited to be told.

'It seems that Titch might have done a bunk, darling.'

'I thought she was in the playroom.'

'Yes, we all did. Someone left the door open; she might have nipped out of the dining-room window.'

'She was never a cat who liked to stay in at night: too much the mouser.' As she spoke, Sarah began to look vaguely around the room, stooping to peer under the bed and half-opening a wardrobe door. 'All right,' she said, 'we'd better make sure. Close the dining-room window' (this to James), 'and we'll have a proper search.'

Half-an-hour later it had become quite obvious that the cat was nowhere in the house. Jemima had gone out of the french window into the garden, taking with her Titch's bowl and a handful of the cat-food nuggets that Titch was particularly fond of; she tapped a fork against the side of the plate and let the nuggets trickle across her palm so that they rattled against the china; she called 'Titch-Titch-Titch', waiting a moment then calling again or tapping with the fork. At every moment, she expected to see the lithe, black shape break through the shrubbery at the top of the garden with a long bound and run silently across the lawn into the oasis of yellow light, offering the little *Puurrrp* of delight, so like the ringing tone of a telephone, then walking a sinuous back along Jemima's shin, nuzzling her with her head and flicking with her stiff tail. 'Come on Titch,' Jemima would say, holding the bowl of food just above the cat's head as she retreated into the room. 'Come on,' and she would put the food down on the dining-room floor, even though that had been forbidden while they lived there, so that she could close the french window while Titch rummaged in the bowl. Then she would go out into the hall and shout, 'It's all right, I've got her,' and everyone would come downstairs asking 'Where was she?' or 'Well done, Jemima', or 'Oh, I'm so relieved, what would we have done if she hadn't turned up?'

But it didn't happen. The others came into the dining-room and George asked, 'Any luck?'

'She won't come; I don't know where she is.' Jemima put the bowl down outside, close to the house, and came in.

'I wouldn't leave the food out, Jemima. She's more likely to come back if she's hungry. If she came back during the night, she would eat it all and perhaps go off again.'

Jemima retrieved the bowl and set it down on the carpet, just as she had done in the fantasy where she found Titch. 'Will she be hungry in the morning?' she asked. 'Suppose she catches a mouse and eats it?' And she clenched her fists and started to cry.

George Morrison had been working and living in Bristol for six years. The twins could just remember arriving at the new house: the excitement of it all, having a garden for the first time, having stairs and a front door with a porch and, best of all, being told that they could have a cat. George had brought her home a couple of weeks later: a tiny thing, entirely black except for a cravat of white and a white

smudge on one forepaw. George and Sarah liked to think
that Titch had been a token of good luck, since their life in
Bristol had been entirely happy. Moving from the flat in
London had pleased them both. George's new job had
enabled them to do that: had given them a much-improved
standard of living, the kind of environment they wanted for
the twins and the kind of life they wanted for themselves.
They were a mild couple, communicating their level-
headedness, tranquil ways and undemanding fondness for
each other to their children. The news that George's firm
was transferring him to a branch in Manchester had per-
turbed them a little, but after George had been up to see the
house and to investigate the local schools, he was able to
return and report that the new place was bigger and better
than their semi-detached in Bristol, that the garden was
half-as-much space again, that they would be living on the
outskirts of the city — in real countryside, more or less —
and that the twins' new school had an excellent record.
There were sadnesses about leaving Bristol, but these were
more than compensated for by the anticipation of happy
times in Manchester. 'Taking a big step up in the world' was
how George described it to them all.

Now Titch had disappeared and a note of sourness had
crept into things. George and Sarah had finally managed to
get the children to bed, but not before Jemima, whose tears
wouldn't stop, had said, 'It's all your fault — and your silly
job.' They had tried to console her, but she would have
none of it. 'I don't want to leave Bristol. I hate Manchester. I
hate it. Titch doesn't want to go, that's why she's run away.
I want to stay here and have Titch back.' James had been
sullenly silent, accusing without speaking.

'She'll be back in the morning,' George had insisted before switching off the children's bedroom light. 'She always
comes round in the morning to be fed. You mustn't worry.'

'Suppose she hasn't come back by the time we leave?'
Jemima insisted. George hesitated. 'I'm sure she will. Cats

155

get up very early you know.' The twins looked at him over their bedclothes, clearly disbelieving.

'Go to sleep now. She'll turn up tomorrow.' George half-closed the door so that there was a slight glow in the room from the landing light, then went downstairs and poured himself a small whisky. Sarah watched this unusual practice; the Scotch was only for guests and dinner parties and under normal circumstances neither of them took a drink from one week's end to the next. Then she said, 'I think I'll join you.'

They sat in armchairs on either side of the unlit fire and sipped from their glasses like amateurs. Every now and then, George would get up and peer through the window. 'Do you think she will?' Sarah asked. Then, by way of an explanation, 'I heard what you were saying to the twins.'

'I don't know. I expect so, don't you?'

'It's just that I sometimes don't see her for a whole day. She goes off mousing, or whatever she does. Often she comes back to be fed in the evening.'

'Oh, really? Have you any more cheering thoughts to offer? Perhaps she's been run over or catnapped for her fur.' Sarah didn't reply: waiting for the apology.

'I didn't mean to snap; I'm sorry.' It was predictable and comforting. 'It's just that I haven't the first idea how we'll be able to drag them off to Manchester tomorrow if the wretched animal doesn't turn up. Can you imagine it?'

'Yes, I can. Too well. Could one of us stay behind?'

George shook his head. 'There'll be no furniture here; things have to be sorted out at the other house; the kids have to go to school the next morning and I'm due at the branch at eight. Hopeless. Anyway, the estate agent's calling to collect the keys before we set off. No, it's no good. We'll just have to pray that we find her.' He put his drink down, unfinished, and went out into the garden. Sarah watched from the open french window as he paced to and fro across the lawn, calling and making little kissing noises.

A wind had shredded the cloud. An almost full moon lightened the sky to inky-blue, frosting the lawn and the low shrubbery with its frail, metallic light. Apart from George's intermittent, sing-song call, there was silence. Silence, and no movement anywhere.

They were more than half-way to Manchester before one of them spoke: Jemima, who said 'She'll die, won't she?' The girl stared out of the window at the other cars as they nudged alongside, or snapped past on the southbound carriageway. It was as bad, George thought, to have the silence broken as to have it maintained. He felt headachy and tense, unable to concentrate properly on his driving. A gusting cross-wind was making things difficult and the brittle atmosphere in the car kept dragging his mind away from the high-speed business in hand. A few miles back, he had pulled out to overtake and had been made guilty and scared by the flashing lights and the swell and fade of a horn-blast as a Jag, coming up fast in the lane he had suddenly occupied, was made to swerve and pass him with only seconds separating manoeuvre from massacre.

'Someone will take her in; she won't starve. She's a beautiful cat. It won't take her long to find a home where people love her.' As he said it, George realized it was about the worst remark possible.

'I'd sooner she died,' Jemima said tonelessly.

George sighed. His eyes were gritty and he felt as if he had been driving for days. 'Let's take a break,' he suggested. 'It's lunchtime. We'll pull into the next service-station and get some food. We need petrol, anyway.'

Fifteen miles further along the motorway, he angled on to the slip-road and parked the car in the grey wasteland between the restaurant and the petrol pumps. A dank wind swirled over the low, grimy buildings and daytime neon. They settled with their trays at a littered table near a window. George closed his eyes for a couple of seconds, trying

157

to rid himself of the feeling that he was locked into a fixed stare. The motion of the car was in his bones. He felt as if he were floating forward. When he opened his eyes again, they still felt like a pair of peeled grapes. Jemima was peering out of the window, just as she had done in the car.

James poked around on his plate with his knife. Turning away from George and towards Sarah, he said: 'I would rather she died, too; I don't want another family to have her,' and he began to cry, silently, the tears welling and falling straight down into his lap as he leaned forward and put his hand across his forehead. Sarah clutched the boy's shoulder and looked helplessly at George. None of them moved or spoke for a minute or so; then because there was nothing else to do, they ate the cooling, glutinous fry-up on their plates.

It had been Sarah who had finally talked the children out of the garden and into the car. Perhaps she, more than the others, had been prepared for disaster: after all, she spent most of her day at home and knew better than anyone how the cat was likely to behave. Titch, unlike some cats, had a nature that was determined by environment. Inside the house, she was given to sitting on laps, curling up in front of the fire like a chocolate-box decoration, nuzzling and stretching in ecstasy under the ticklings and scratchings administered by the twins, or tucking her forepaws under her chest and sinking into a trance in the heat from a sun-lit window. Once outside the door, however, she was a hunter; dozy domesticity ended at the first fringe of rough grass beyond the lawn. Sarah rather liked that about her: liked the fact that she wasn't always to be found lodged on a windowsill waiting for food, or sleeping the day away on a bed. And she had known, last night, that if Titch was stalking the back-garden wilderness of half a square mile − or whatever constituted her demesne − then it was altogether likely that she wouldn't put in an appearance for some hours: perhaps, even, a day or so. She had been prepared for it, but that didn't make things any easier. She, too, felt the loss.

'We'd better make a move.' George got to his feet and led them out to the car, past the vending machines and rows of beeping electronic games. As he pulled out on to the motorway, it felt like a second departure.

The new house was on the edge of countryside. Detached, impressively gabled and boasting five bedrooms, it really did reflect a change of life-style, a change of status, for the family. There was even a small driveway that bifurcated to serve both front door and garage. High hedges hid the front of the house from view and continued along the boundaries of half an acre of garden.

The removal lorry was somewhere behind them, still on the road and not expected for an hour or two. The family had carried only the suitcases containing their clothes, a cardboard box stuffed with provisions, a few cooking implements and some bedding, wedged in above the cases, to be aired ready for the first night. George pulled up in front of the house. 'Here we are.'

The children looked around gloomily, as their father unlocked the boot and piled its contents on the three low steps that led up to the door. He hefted the cases himself, leaving Sarah to bring the box, while the twins carried sheets and blankets. On the top step, he paused, putting one case down and fumbling for the key. They entered to the brisk, fresh smell of polish, a hallway lit by the soft evening sunlight that poured through a landing window. Titch was running down the newly-carpeted stairway towards them, little crescendos of purring offering a welcome. George sat down heavily on one of the cases and watched the cat nudge and lean against the twins' hands as they knelt on the floor laughing with delight. Afterwards, he worked out that the open landing window had been Titch's entrance to

159

the house; but that was all the logic he could bring to what had happened.

Almost the only remark any of them made about the incident was George's to Sarah, that night, after the twins had gone to bed. He said, 'It's nearly two hundred and fifty miles from Bristol to Manchester, even by a direct motorway route.'

Sarah looked at him. 'That's not quite the point, is it?' She smiled a bewildered smile.

Recollections

When he woke, it was in the dark. For a moment he didn't know where he was. It was an almost palpable darkness, motionless and thick like something clotted. He remembered waking in his grandmother's house in the country, how the deep darkness would slowly lighten to a gleam at the curtain, enabling him to make out the shapes of things: the bedstead, the washstand with its flower-patterned ewer, the mirror flanked by hunting prints and an old photograph of the farmhouse. When he was a child, his parents used to send him there for the long holiday. He loved it more than he could express. The rhythms of farm life, the early waking and early sleeping, the excitement of rising at first light, the sound of pails clanking in the yard and the low snuffle and rustle of the cattle in the milking shed carrying on the still air, the endless vista of trees and fields, the brook, the high pasture where he went with Grandpa to gather mushrooms for breakfast, the return to a smell of frying bacon, crossing to the kitchen door past the loose boxes so that he could give a sugar lump to Major, the old pensioned-off carthorse, and to Sweep, his grandfather's riding horse, whose blunt, oddly bashful, cobby face would regard him dolefully as he fumbled in his pocket

161

for the morning treat . . . these things never ceased to bring him pure pleasure. Long after he had grown to manhood, after he had married, after the children had left to follow their own lives, he thought about those summers at the farm and wondered why he had settled for a life of drab routine in the city.

He supposed that, in part, it had to do with facility versus inclination. He hadn't been born to farming or to country ways. He and his parents had always lived in the city, where his father's small accountancy firm could flourish. Like his father, he had proved 'good at figures'; his career had taken him to the position of Company Secretary with a wealthy manufacturing concern and he was able to enjoy the extra benefits — car, lengthy holidays, free medical insurance and the rest — in addition to a considerable salary. Two of the children had been privately educated, he had bought a large house in one of the most pleasant sub-urbs: life had been kind, that much was undeniable. Also undeniable was the fact that it hadn't really been the life he had wanted. Couldn't he have broken out — given it a try, summoned the courage to take a risk, to start again, to have woken each morning to that immutable beauty coming into focus as the sky lightened, rather than to the blare and grime and false, chemical warmth of city streets? Why not?

Well, there had been money to consider, and opportun-ity, the children's education and welfare; and then, of course, there had been Grace. He was very fond of Grace, just as she was fond of him. They had lived a mild and contented life together, rarely squabbling, rarely disagree-ing. They demanded little of each other, but gave much. In twenty-eight years of marriage, no disenchantment or dis-affection, no passing jealousy or resentment had been strong enough to drive a wedge between them. Their attrac-tion to each other had been founded on a quiet, loving, easy-going and oddly passionless view of the world and of each other. Their marriage had built on that foundation. But

Grace would never – could never – have shared the life he sometimes dreamed of. Yes, there had been Grace to think of, too.

He always carried with him, though, the memories of Spinney Farm. Memories only; except for the one, small concession he forced life to grant him. It wasn't much – a pretty tenuous link with the life he had lost, the life he had never really had. It was at the farm, as a child, that he had learned to ride. It started with Sunday afternoon jaunts, trundling round the paddock on Major, his Grandpa walking alongside in case he had to be caught. Then there had been more thrilling rides on Sweep, sitting in front of Grandpa, who gripped him around the waist with one sinewy arm while they cantered. He had known, at once, that this was something he had to have for himself: this feeling of freedom and excitement, with just a touch of danger. He pleaded, he cajoled, he made promises to forgo his pocket money for life; and, finally, a part of holidaying at Spinney Farm was regular lessons and two full rides a week from a nearby stable. From that moment, all through his childhood and adult life, he had ridden regularly, kept it as a hobby – or rather, that was the word Grace and the kids and friends at work had for it. Secretly, he never thought of riding that way. He was truly alive, he thought, when he was on horseback; the sense of being free, of being un-trammelled, of being apart from a world of figures and balance sheets and policies and promotions, the sense of himself, was as fresh now, at fifty-five, as it had always been. He loved all aspects of riding: schooling, hacking, hunting, trail-riding in the Scottish Borders or dressage in the south London indoor school he attended; all had their different thrills and disciplines. He enjoyed the grooming and feeding, the smell of the tack-room, the rows of polished saddles and bridles.

He still rode once a week, at least. Grace would chuckle about it. 'You're getting to be an old man, now,' she would sometimes say, as he set off in jodhpurs and boots each Saturday morning, 'you'll have to think about changing to bowls or an occasional leisurely game of cribbage at the pub.' Behind the banter, he knew, lay a slight concern. She had always worried that he might come to grief one day. Her only visit to the stables had been a brief one, when she had stayed out of the way of the horses in case they might bite or kick and had stood well clear of the string as they set off for an hour's ride in the park. 'Why not at least give up hunting?' she had asked. 'Some of those fences look awfully big.'

He had merely smiled and made a vague promise for the future without having the slightest intention of keeping it. 'One day, perhaps. I've got a few years yet, I reckon. Anyway, it's the horse that does the jumping, you know; all I have to do is sit there.'

It had been raining: a bad day, the ground treacherous and very gooey, hard on the horses and hard on the riders too. The sky was slate-grey and low. A sharp, gusting wind carried thongs of needling drizzle with it that seemed to scratch and roughen the riders' faces. For the first hour or so, he had gone reasonably well, ignoring the discomfort which, after all, wasn't something new to him, and taking few if any chances at the jumps. There came a point, though, when he started to tire; the horse was tired, too, and maybe the unsureness of his mount transmitted itself. His control lost some of its fineness as the going became heavier; his horse wallowed at some of the jumps and then, at a particularly bad hedge and ditch, fell. He came out over the horse's neck, landing heavily, and the animal was on top of him before he could make any move to get clear.

After that, everything had been shadowy – dim and very far off. He was aware of voices as a just-audible hum, like the fluctuating note of a generator. There were lights, harsh or muted, illuminating surfaces that always seemed smooth and pale and distant. He was aware of darkness and light, night and day, but couldn't tell how many times each had come and gone. There were moments of silence, of blankness, that could have been seconds or days; and when he returned from these elisions it was to a world, a life, that seemed to be taking place somewhere near to him, but not there, where he was. Touch and sight, smell and hearing, were almost completely in abeyance, but he had little sense of loss, little desire to strive towards those things. Coddled in a fog of near-nerveless disconnection, he floated like jetsam in a warm sea, beyond confusion, beyond fear. The unpredictable moments of absence took him from even that slightness. Then, a time came when he returned from one such gap to what seemed a dream: there was a vividness about things, a particularity, that wasn't part of the twilight world he had been inhabiting.

His sight cleared a little and he thought he must be in a garden, or some cultivated place. The air was fresh and warm and he had a sense of colour just at the furthest edge of his vision. He was on a lawn, lying still, but able to see, beneath an arc of blue sky, a small wooden bridge and the flutter of sunlight on water. Beyond the bridge, things were indistinct. He could hear, nearby, the lulling, soft, *rip rip rip* of a horse cropping grass. It occurred to him that he should, in a minute, quite soon, though there was no hurry, stroll down to the bridge and cross it, to see if it was safe for the horse and whether there was pasture on the other side and land to ride over.

He remembered that, he remembered all these things, as he woke in the dark, not knowing where he was. Then, in the next instant, he did know; he was awake and aware and alive and he knew. His hands shot upwards in a reflex of fear, the fingernails scrabbling and tearing at the lid of the coffin, splinters spearing the flesh, gouging his finger-ends into a soft, gory mess as he fought. His back arched and he screamed a scalding, harsh, scream — unbearable for

165

its bald terror, unhinged, unheard. His heart crashed and crashed beneath his ribs, like a series of detonations.

Grace switched off the gas and took the egg from the saucepan, rolling it from hand to hand until she reached the table and plopped it into the egg-cup. She was still in her black; she hadn't even bothered to remove her coat. She sat down at the table and buttered a slice of bread. The house seemed unnaturally quiet. The crunch of her egg-spoon on the shell was a spade going into gravel. It was her first meal alone, in the evening, in their house; she realized how much it would hurt her to eat alone, to cook only for herself. Tomorrow she would clear his things up: his papers and clothes, his boots and mackintosh and hat from the hallway, and put them somewhere out of sight. She couldn't think how life might become bearable again. She pushed the egg away and stared down at the table. She wanted to cry, but there was no crying left in her that day.